I0578635

LOVE, AUSTEN

A CLEAN FAKE RELATIONSHIP ROMANCE

BRITNEY M. MILLS

CRYSTAL CANYON PRESS

Copyright © 2018 by Britney M Mills

Cover design by Blue Valley Author Services

All rights reserved.

No part of this book may be reproduced in any form or by any electronic or mechanical means, including information storage and retrieval systems, without written permission from the author, except for the use of brief quotations in a book review.

To Max
for inspiring me to follow me dreams.

CHAPTER 1

$\mathcal{M}$eg Austen heard the computer humming its startup song as she sorted the envelopes at her desk. A couple of pieces of junk mail and several bills. Twisting a piece of her blond hair, she considered leaving the envelopes untouched. Maybe if she blinked fast enough, they'd disappear. She loved to see what came in the mailbox as a kid, but now she understood that with the postman usually came papers demanding money, a never-ending battle.

She didn't have to open the letters to know what they said. Past-Due in red ink. The costs of remodeling and renting a physical building weren't things she'd had to worry about before, but her growing matchmaking business had stretched her bank account thinner than she'd ever seen it. Ramen noodles was a staple in her apartment now.

One envelope stood out from the pile, its square shape sticking up next to the rest. These were the letters she wanted to receive. The ones printed on linen or parchment or mylar, the words in an elegant script. Pulling the sharp letter opener from her desk drawer, she sliced open the envelope and pulled out the contents.

Meg skimmed past the names of the bride's parents to find Rebecca Ann spelled out in a swoopy script. Her husband-to-be was Richard Story, one of the three matches Meg had picked out for her. Included was a picture of the happy couple sitting on a park bench, gazing into each other's eyes.

This. Everything about this validated why she did what she did. That look on his face as he stared at her. Rebecca's wide smile. Totally worth the hours of research it took to compile the data to find people their best match.

She stood, turning to the wall at her right. Covering the wall were dozens of invitations with the engagement pictures taped next to them. The success stories of the Love, Austen Matchmaking Company over the past four years.

A sharp pain sliced through her chest, envy trickling in its wake. Her life was better than she could have hoped, near perfect by certain standards. She owned a business she adored, had amazing friends, and all the Nutella hot chocolate she could drink from the creperie around the corner from the new building.

The only thing she was missing was the kind of relationship her best friend Lily had with her fiancé, Ben. With their wedding on the horizon, Meg's life would change, as she'd depended on Lily for so many things. Marriage changed friendships and while she had been trying to prepare herself for it over the past several months, she could only hope she'd find peace from it all.

Taping the newest invitation to the wall, she glanced at the envelopes again, knowing she'd have to tackle them before lunch, or they'd sit there for weeks. She arranged them on the corner of her desk and clicked on her email inbox. Several new emails from current and potential clients waited and as she scanned the headlines, her eyes stopped on one of them.

Her stomach did a flip as she read: INVESTMENT REQUEST. With a quick click, she scrolled down faster than she could even comprehend. She hadn't learned anything from her attempt at speed reading and rolled the page back to the top.

"Dear Miss Austen,

We thank you for your application to the Boston Investors Alliance. We have gone through your profile and request more information about your company before moving forward."

Not one to object to reading the end of a book, her eyes slid to the last paragraph.

"Please give our office a call between 9:00 am-5:00 pm in the next day or two. Ask for Mark Allred."

Her hand hovered over the receiver as she stared at the wall in front of her.

Should I call them now?

She scanned to see what time they sent the email. Forty-seven minutes ago. Was that too soon to respond? Would they think she was desperate?

What was a little humiliation? It had almost killed her pride to send in the application in the first place. She'd made a goal to depend on herself for any need, business or other-wise, the day she found out her mother had taken half of her college savings.

After a coaxing debate from her assistant Tiffany, she'd decided that getting a business loan, or taking on investors, wasn't like robbing a bank. Besides, people had the guts to convince investors on TV that their product would make millions. Sending in an electronic application made her grateful she didn't have to beg and plead in front of an audience.

Nervous energy bubbled in her stomach, and she shook her hands to calm herself for a moment.

They can say no. I'll just find another way to do things. Just breathe.

She picked up the phone, dialing the number at the bottom of the email.

"Boston Investors Alliance. How may I direct your call?" a woman's voice came over the line.

"Um… that's a good question." The name already escaped her, and she had to skim the email, seeing the information she needed, "May I speak to Mark Allred, please?"

"One moment, please."

Meg heard the click, and then that awful trumpet, trying-to-be-jazz type music filled her ears. She pulled the phone away and rolled her eyes. If they were going to play music, why couldn't they play something most people listened to?

Once the call connected, the ringing tone echoed in Meg's ear, sending her mind into doubt. She'd gained experience with talking to people of various economic backgrounds in the time she'd been running Love, Austen, but the thought of some unknown person deciding whether to give her money based on a few questions from an application formed knots in her stomach.

Her finger hovered over the disconnect button, giving herself to the count of ten. When she reached eight, a male voice answered, causing her mind to scramble as it focused on his words. Her stomach gurgled, and dryness overtook her mouth.

Chocolate. She'd need some of that when this call finished.

After quick introductions, the raspy voice on the line said, "I'm looking at your file now. With all the information of your background, your business plan, and everything else you've submitted, you've passed the first stage of the process. We feel it's important to vet each client before handing out money." He paused and Meg hoped it wasn't to drive the point home. She wasn't giving up now. "The board requested a phone interview, to discover why you want people to invest in your company. There's only so much we can learn on paper."

The line went silent, and Meg pursed her lips, unsure what to do. Was he waiting for her to answer? Or was this another pause? Her heart raced, and she placed a hand over it, hoping to calm it enough to breathe in a few mouthfuls of air without sounding like she'd just run a 5K.

"Well, sir, I've been working on Love, Austen since my senior year of college, so almost five years. In that time, we've been able to grow our clientele each year, this last year by nearly thirty-three percent, many coming from referrals of past clients. Our success rate of couples still together after the first year has been steady for most of that time and in the last year, rose another six percent."

Mr. Allred said nothing. Twisting the cord at the base of her receiver, Meg tried not to breathe loudly into it.

"What would our investment go toward?"

She visualized the online application where she'd detailed her answer to that exact question. Closing her eyes, she said, "Well, sir, we've just opened our first physical location on Beacon Street, giving us the adequate room for meeting potential clients as well as bringing in some of the locals. But my overall vision for this company is to go global. After meeting with a business analyst, he suggested we increase our online footprint. My priority is to design an app allowing people to benefit from all the conveniences of our company from anywhere around the world."

"Ah, those applications my grandkids talk about. I'm

lucky I know how to text. Don't get me started about those smiley faces." The man chuckled, and a pity laugh escaped from her lips.

Great. My future rests in the hands of a man who doesn't understand technology. It was the very basis of her business in the way she calculated personality traits and compatibility scores to match her clients. She tried to picture the man, probably nearing retirement at a job he'd held for at least forty years. Comfort was his signature.

The thought sparked an idea and she said, "Yes, but we want to make it user-friendly. Something people can use no matter their skill level with technology. We match couples from age eighteen up as high as eighty so far. We at Love, Austen believe that everyone should have a chance at love, and for some, even a second."

The man let out a sigh. "That's a great sentiment, and I'm interested to see the inner-workings of your business. My question for you, Miss Austen, is how much do you trust in your matching program?"

"Excuse me?"

"Do you have a boyfriend, husband, or significant other?"

She opened her mouth but found the air too thick to swallow. The closest thing to a boyfriend was the stock photo in the silver frame Tiffany had given her for her last birthday. Her family was almost non-existent, and her life was her business, making it difficult for picture-worthy moments.

"Boyfriend? I have a… boy-friend." She smacked herself on the forehead, hoping he hadn't heard it. Liquid slurping echoed from the other end, and she frowned. She was sweating over a simple word, and he was smacking his lips in her ear.

Mr. Allred cleared his throat and said, "Perfect. We look forward to meeting him."

Another pause on the line sent Meg's mind into overdrive. What had she been thinking? Did they expect her to run all the numbers and matching for said boyfriend as well? She pictured some men she'd met wanting to be matched in the last few months and found herself cringing to think of even holding their hands.

Sound came from the other line again, pulling her back to the present. "For our company to get an overall picture of your business, we will be sending someone to look at the place, your processes, and any other details we might need to consider. If you have any special events coming up, please notify our office. Client experiences are valuable to the final decision, and we weigh those considerably higher than the basic information. We hope to have an answer to you in the next thirty days."

"You'll come to my office?" Why was her brain moving in slow motion?

"Yes, like I said before, we like to get the overall picture rather than just the numbers on paper."

Thirty days. One month. She picked up the unopened envelopes. They symbolized money lost. An urgency to start development on the app right away hit her, just as it had every day over the past six months. Her account balance showed little of her scrimping habits and as she thought about it, thirty days was much better than having to save for the next ten to twenty years.

"Okay. Call me when your people will be by."

Hanging up the phone, Meg laid her head on the desk, lifting and dropping it, repeating the action a few times. Who said doing something she loved wouldn't feel like work?

CHAPTER 2

$\mathcal{L}$eaning back in his desk chair, Parker Matthews rubbed at his eyes. He'd been looking at the financial numbers of one of his clients for the past fifteen minutes, and he hadn't made any progress; everything seeming to blend together. As he gazed out the window, he saw a navy sky and a few lights on in the building next door. He'd arrived at the office of his law firm before six that morning, the first rays of sun not even over the horizon at that time.

Checking the time on his phone, he saw an eleven. So that's why his brain wasn't functioning. The walls were constricting, and he wished there were some signal to what he needed to find so he could go home. The verified numbers had to be sent in by morning if he wanted to keep the momentum on this case to continue.

Just as he bent to study the numbers again, he heard a knock on his open door. Bart Brooks, one of the partners of the firm, sauntered in.

"Working late again?"

With a sly smile, Parker said, "No, I'm just really early for tomorrow. What are you doing here so late?"

"My wife's out of town until Friday, so I'm trying to get as much done as I can before she gets back. She hates it when I work late and with the Christensen case, I feel like I'm pounding up against a brick wall to get the facts straight." Bart took a seat in one of the leather chairs in front of Parker's desk.

"That must have been your reheated pasta alfredo I smelled." Parker leaned back, intertwining his fingers and using them to cradle his head.

Bart nodded, his nose turned up. "One of the tough parts about her being gone is I don't get to eat her cooking. What are you working on?"

Sliding a hand through his short, brown hair, Parker said, "The verifications in the Murphy case. It's been a rough one. They've bought and sold so many things over their years together, they can't remember it all clearly."

"Good luck with that." Bart leaned back, resting his head back on top of the chair. His eyes turned to the ceiling, his mouth opening and closing several times before he spoke again. "I thought I'd let you know, you're in the running for partner."

Parker snorted. "Just in the running? Bart, it's to fill my father's position. What's there to consider?" The heat crept up his neck and into his ears, blood thrumming in them. Sure, he thought he'd be a shoo-in for the position, as it was his father who'd helped start the firm.

"Now, hold on a minute. It hasn't been long since you lost your father, and I know how hard it's been. And as someone who's watched you grow up from a toddler, I'm rooting for you too. But the board selected three candidates."

"Who are the other two then?" Unable to sit any longer,

Parker stood, pacing back and forth between his desk and the large mahogany shelves along the wall.

Bart faked a smile and said, "Sharon Teller and Connor Simpson."

Throwing his hands into the air, Parker looked at the older man, the words not forming completely on his tongue. "What… Are they serious?"

"One more thing…" Bart held up his finger and waited for Parker to stop mumbling. Parker's gut and Bart's expression told him he wouldn't like what came next. "Do you remember that woman who gave you a black eye because you tried to push her chair in?"

"How could I forget? I got a twenty-minute lecture from her about the role of women in society today, plus a severe warning from Todd about distance." Parker could see the scene so clearly as it was only six months before. He'd tried to help the opposing spouse scoot her chair in when it had become stuck on a loose piece of carpet in the conference room. He'd nearly lost the case because of it. "Bart, stop stalling. That can't have anything to do with being chosen."

"This is a tough job, and we don't always look like the good guys. As a partner, you'd have extra responsibilities, extra attention. I'm not supposed to tell you this, but my suggestion is to find a date, who can turn into a long-term date."

"Like a girlfriend?" Parker scrunched his nose. Balling up a fist, he swung to punch the wall but pulled back before making contact. It seemed an ironic requirement for a partner of a divorce law firm.

Bart leaned forward, clearing his throat. "A girlfriend with marriage potential. You're going to need someone you can talk to you, especially after some of the cases you've gone through. Someone you can trust to help you make sense of it all. Remind you on occasion that you're not a bad guy."

Parker's mind was still caught up on the thought of a girl-friend. "Do you remember what happened to the last girl I proposed to? Is this some sick joke?" Parker took two steps and slumped down in his seat. Exhaustion hit him like a wall, his eyelids now heavy, while his mind worked to process the new information.

Bart's face sobered. "I do, Parker. I remember it. But you've moved on; you're stronger now. You know the signs."

"Yeah, I know the signs that a woman is about to leave me five minutes before she actually does. Suitcases overflowing with clothes. Mom leaves. I'm on one knee, and my ex-girl-friend says she's taking a job across the country. Bye, Court-ney." Fury welled up in his chest as his mind relived the still painful moments.

With a sad smile, Bart gave him a curt nod. "Look, son. It's been hard, but you're a handsome guy, a great lawyer, and a loyal friend. You've had a few bad experiences. That doesn't mean you should give up altogether. As a friend, I wanted you to hear it from me. If you want to take your father's place, start there."

"What other tests are there?" A web of frustration wound around his mind as he realized his appointment to partner wouldn't be a slam dunk based on his last name.

"Find yourself a girl first. We hope to finalize the appointment by the end of the month." He stood, his expres-sion somber.

Looking down at his watch, the date read April second. So, he'd have twenty-nine days to find a girl and prove he deserved partner. Make that twenty-seven days since it was a short month and almost the third.

"I guess the worst I can do is give it a try." Parker gave Bart a close-lipped smile as he stood, reaching forward his arm to grasp the other man's outstretched hand.

"I know you can do it, Parker. I was there when your

mother left. It devastated your father but look how he rebounded with Heather."

At such a callous summary of his life, Parker could only nod, trying to swallow the mound blocking his airway. His mother's voice rang in his head as it had for the past twelve years. "I'll sign whatever you need me to for you to keep the kids. I'm gone, and I won't be coming back."

This was why he didn't date women. They always left. Always.

CHAPTER 3

*M*eg adjusted the top of her dress, wishing it weren't strapless or teal. Just a slight wind blew from the air conditioner, and all the hairs on her arms stood up. A shrug or even a shawl would be perfect for the occasion, at least until she had to walk down the aisle. As much as she loved her roommate and best friend, she knew it was best to just let her have her day, no matter how much suffering was involved.

At least the wedding and reception are indoors. Winter hadn't quite given up its hold on the city, evidenced by Meg's complexion. She frowned as she looked at the difference of her skin compared to the color of the dress. Teal was for girls who didn't burn when out in the sun for more than fifteen minutes.

Doors swung open behind her, letting in another wave of cool air. Crossing her arms over her chest, she rubbed her upper arms, hoping to get rid of the goosebumps along her skin. Meg turned to see her best friend walk in, pin curls and braids pulled back into a stunning updo.

"You are beautiful, dear friend." The two girls embraced.

"Perfect dress, second-perfect venue, and near-perfect groom."

"Yes to the perfect dress, which only fits because you found another venue before I consumed gallons of ice cream stress-eating. As far as the near-perfect groom..." Lily moved to take a seat on one of the mauve sofa chairs. "He is definitely that. Hampshire House refunded our deposit, and Ben said the fire took out four of the five floors."

Meg's head still ached when she thought of the whirlwind to find and secure a venue with two weeks until the wedding. Thank goodness for clients who had connections in the city. "What are best friends for? Now, let's get you into this dress so you can get hitched."

"What do you think of your dress?"

Meg turned her focus to the white dress hanging next to the large, gilded mirror, hoping to hide her awful poker face. "It's great. But it's you we want everyone looking at."

Pulling the dress off the hanger, she said, "Arms up!" and pulled the dress down, doing her best to avoid snagging any pins on its way over Lily's hair. She got to work on pulling and tugging on the corset and then the long line of buttons just below it.

"You'd think that I'd have learned how to expertly cinch a corset by now." Meg pulled on the strings in back, trying to make them as tight as possible before moving onto the next loops. She hoped they wouldn't break now.

Lily chuckled. "Since you wear them every day, of course." Meg smacked her shoulder as she held what felt like reins in the other.

"We should invent something to get the look of the corset but have it feel like you're wearing sweats. We'd call it the corseat or sworset." Lily's laughter caused a moment of sadness to sweep over Meg, knowing this was one of the last times she'd have her best friend so easy and free. As great as many people claimed marriage to be, there were still more challenges and heightened stress than just taking care of oneself.

"Did you hit your head or something?" Tying the strings in a bow, Meg laughed. "Sweats wouldn't look good in your pictures today. Besides, I'm not untying this cupcake wrapper now that I've got it all done up."

Lily turned, smiling. She was radiant. The sadness turned into that darn ache from when Meg had seen the wedding invitation, settling in her chest once again. She'd felt it a few times in the past year, but the more frequent occurrences signaled maybe her heart was trying to tell her something. It was a stab of loneliness, and Meg wasn't even sure it would go away this time.

She focused on the girl in front of her. Her best friend was getting married, on Meg's own recommendation. The change was enough to dredge up the random thoughts to her mind that many people asked her in their first consultation.

Would she ever marry? What would she be like as a wife? Her mother's face popped into her mind, the poster woman for leaving chaos in her wake. Her relationships lasted about as long as a gallon of milk. Meg's own track record caused her to wonder if maybe relationship woes were genetic.

Focus. Maid of honor duties. Find a boyfriend.

How tacky was it to find someone at a wedding? Desperate times. With only a few weeks until the decision and no idea when the BIA would be sending people to check out her company, she needed to start the search yesterday.

"Five minutes!" Meg didn't have to turn to know it was Lily's mother Jill. The woman embraced her daughter, a tender scene Meg would never share with her own mother.

Jill then wrapped Meg in a hug and whispered, "Thank you for always being there for her."

Surprised by the tingle in her nose and sudden lump in

her throat, Meg swiped her finger under her eyes when they pulled apart.

"Now, Jill. We haven't even started the ceremony. Don't start the water works just yet." They both laughed as they sniffled, dabbing at the tears before it ruined their makeup.

Lily turned to Meg and smiled, biting the inside of her cheek as she did so. Nerves.

"Showtime. You'll do amazing. Just remember that you and Ben fit together like ice and water." Meg winced, realizing her ability to use similes hadn't gotten better over the past decade.

With an upturned eyebrow, Lily responded, "So, we're both really cold people?"

Meg bit her lip. "Okay, you know I'm not the best at comparisons off the cuff. You just mesh well. I'm so happy for you." Someone pulled at her arm. "And, now I've got to go. Congrats!"

CHAPTER 4

*L**ongest procession ever.*

As Parker counted the number of couples who'd already come down the aisle, he wondered if the bride would ever make her way to the altar. As the musicians started the song over again, he was ready to gouge his eyes out. It was one thing to be at a wedding, it was another to feel like a bystander at a parade, although some saltwater taffy would've been nice right then.

Staring up into the rafters, he plotted ways to speed things up. The only idea that came to mind was to put a lighter next to the sprinkling system or pull the fire alarm. But then again, the bride would never forgive him. He'd only met her a few times, but he knew all the drama around having to move the ceremony due to a fire at what some of the women had called the "Jane Austen Reception Hall" because of its older charms. Better to sit still instead of forever being called he-who-ruined-the-wedding.

He turned to see the progress of the next couple and found the girl in a different style dress from the rest of the bridesmaids. Maid of honor? Looking to the guy next to her,

Parker recognized Drew, Ben's younger brother and best man. Switching his eyes back to the girl, he studied her.

Not an expert at fashion, even he could see the teal dress wasn't the best cut to her frame. But as he gazed up to her face, he felt a wave of goosebumps travel up his arm. Her hair was twisted to the side, and her small, upturned nose fit the delicate features of her face. But seeing her blue-green eyes pricked something in his chest, like he'd poked himself with a needle.

A small pop sound came from the ground, and Parker looked down, seeing the teal runner bunch up next to his row. Her high heel caught, and she tried to free it with a roll of her ankle. Drew pulled her forward another step, but the heel didn't break free.

Her momentum shot backwards, and time slowed down as her arms flailed in the air, sending the bouquet flying several feet above. As if on instinct, Parker reached out his arms and caught her inches above the ground. Adrenaline poured through him as his breathing sped up.

Peering at her face, he found her eyes closed and her face scrunched, bracing for impact, no doubt. When she did open them, the gold and green flecks in the blue sea of her eyes hypnotized him.

"Are you all right?" he asked after what seemed like minutes.

She turned her head and as he looked up, he found dozens of eyes watching them. The room was silent, even that annoying song had stopped playing. Everyone holding their breath for what would happen next. *Is this what it feels like to be on a reality TV show?*

In one quick moment, the girl jerked up, the movement causing her to slide out of his hands and onto the ground. She reached up to grab onto Drew's arm and made it to her feet. Parker bit back a smile as Drew seemed to be oblivious to the whole scene. He studied her face, noting the rapid change of emotions as she locked eyes with him. She nodded, giving him the faintest of smiles before pulling Drew forward to the altar.

The musicians changed their tune, for which Parker was grateful. At least they were making progress with the whole ceremony. As he looked back at the maid of honor standing next to the altar, a pink flushed her cheeks as he caught her gaze on him. As she looked away, tilting her chin up a few inches, Parker shifted in his seat. This wedding was finally getting interesting.

CHAPTER 5

*E*ntering the same hall from the nuptials two hours before, it surprised Meg at the transformation in such a short time. Teal sashes adorned the white chairs and sat around large round tables draped with white tablecloths. The centerpieces focused on small portraits of Ben and Lily, which Lily had painted herself.

Meg smiled as she saw a few people lean over to touch them. Even after several years of living together, it still amazed her how Lily made her art so lifelike. She just hoped her best friend would find a way to make it profitable, especially after all that went into each piece.

Seeing a few bits of torn paper on the floor, she bent to pick them up. When she stood, she was inches away from the tall stranger, the one who'd saved her from a concussion earlier that day. The smell of apples and cinnamon drifted to her nose. Did guys really smell like that? His grin sent a chill running across her shoulders, and she took a step back, placing her hands on her hips.

"May I help you?"

He stuffed one hand into his pants pocket. "Just trying to

find where I'm supposed to sit." His other arm swung out. "Is there a way to find out without having to go table by table? How many guests are there?"

Picking up the packet of paper from the table next to her, Meg glanced down, trying to avoid his piercing gaze once more. It was bad enough he'd caught her staring at him during the procession. She didn't need him to think she was some crazy whacko. With all the people listed by last name and their table number next to it, Meg was ready for his question. "Name?"

"Parker Matthews." The lower octave of his voice made Meg want to curl up in it.

Nope. She wouldn't do this. Sure, the suit he wore looked like it had been sewn on him, showing off the strong arms and V-shaped upper body. His jawline was what some of her clients requested when filling out their test to be matched. And his ice-blue eyes seemed to shine out even more against the chocolate-brown hair, cut short on the sides.

What was she doing? She looked down at her sheet, sure she wouldn't find his name, since she'd typed up the list herself. After blinking a few times, she found it, right there under M. Matthews, Parker.

"Table two. Over there." She pointed to the table in front and left of the main table. He nodded and started in that direction. Before he got too far, she called out, "Thank you… for earlier."

At first, she didn't think he heard her. But he looked over his shoulder and smiled. "No problem," he said, not breaking stride. Her eyes drifted from his face. She jumped when a voice came from behind her.

"That one looks good from any angle." Meg agreed before she realized she'd been staring at his backside. She turned to find Lily's aunt smiling at her.

Wrapping the older woman in a tight hug, she said, "Aunt Bernice. How was your drive?"

"It was lovely. Spring usually is in New Hampshire. Are you sure you're not ready to move to the country?"

Meg laughed. "As much as I'd love to escape the city once in a while, I don't know if I'd survive that far right now without internet. Love, Austen is going through some growing pains and if I'm not careful, the little campfires will turn into wildfires."

"Well, you'd better make time to come visit. I miss having you girls around, in the summers most of all." During college, Lily and Meg had spent weeks with Bernice, enjoying the time off after exams and relishing the quiet life outside the city. If she could hide out there and still get the investors to approve her, she'd leave right after the wedding.

Squeezing Bernice's hand, Meg nodded. "I will. A weekend at the cabin sounds amazing, especially after all this wedding hubbub."

"I better not keep you," Bernice said, pointing near the head table. "It looks like that tall drink of water is still eyeing you. He's a good-looking one, that's for sure. If you play your cards right, you might be saying your own vows soon." She was gone before Meg voiced an answer.

Before her defenses resisted, Meg turned to see him smiling once again. Who was he? Flynn Rider? She'd have to make sure he had an off-day. She wouldn't let this guy think he was the best thing since streaming TV.

CHAPTER 6

What did people love about weddings? Parker sat at table two, wishing he could be home, watching the opening day of the Red Sox. He'd checked his phone just before he walked into the building, but they were still only in the first inning, score zero, zero.

Instead, he watched as people hugged in all directions, saying, "This is so exciting" or "It's about time those two got hitched." Give those people two weeks, and they'd be asking when the newlyweds would have children.

This whole scene could have been a part of his life. He remembered picking up his grandmother's ring from his father the night before proposing to Courtney. His stepmother Heather had been so excited, saying something like, "Finally!"

His father's skepticism hit him hard every time the memories resurfaced.

"Make sure you know where she stands before you commit for life."

Even now, Parker could feel the frustration he'd felt as he

tried to get his father to be happy for him. "We've been dating for almost three years, Dad. I'm sure."

"And when you both graduate law school in a couple weeks?"

"She's gotten a few job offers here in town."

"But which one did she commit to?" Picturing his father's face as he stared at his son out of the corner of his eye, Parker wished he could be here now.

"Maybe he'd be able to find me a girlfriend." He didn't realize he'd said it aloud until the chair next to him pulled out, and a young brunette sat down.

She smiled at him and said, "Looking for a girlfriend?" The white teeth next to her dark-tanned skin looked almost comical.

"Oh, uh, sorry. I was just having one of those internal arguments."

Sipping from a small water glass on the table, she said, "Who won?"

Parker raised an eyebrow. "I guess I did?"

"Sorry, I'm Ashley Bartlett. I'm best friends with Ben's younger sister Stephanie."

"Parker Matthews, long-time friend of Ben." Feeling the dryness in his mouth, Parker reached for his own glass of water.

Several others sat down at the table, and the room was nearly full. The wedding party moved forward to take their seats at the head table and then a loud cheer rang out as Ben and Lily made their way through the crowd and to their place. As Lily's father took the microphone, Parker leaned over to Ashley.

"I'm assuming you know who most of these people are. Care to share their connections with the newlyweds?" Watching her face transform with excitement, Parker realized he must have hit on the thing she loved the most. As much as he tried not to, his eyes kept glancing in the maid of honor's direction. What better way to find out more about her than talking about the rest of the group as well.

Ashley scooted her chair closer, settling her hand on his forearm. It was casual, but he'd been around people enough to read their intentions. This was just the work of a flirty woman who was way too young for him.

"Okay, so the one on the end to the right is Stephanie and then next to her is Drew. He's the middle child and Ben's best man." She went into more detail than Parker cared to know about Ben's younger brother, but he was the one who'd asked.

Drew got up around that time to give his speech, and Parker had to bite the sides of his cheeks to keep from laughing. Ashley stopped talking the moment she heard his voice, and she didn't blink for the entire four-minute speech. Waiters delivered their salad, and the girl who'd tripped during the ceremony stood, her hand shaking a bit as she took the microphone from Drew.

"Good evening, everyone. I'm Meg Austen, maid of honor. I don't have much to add to what's been said about this amazing couple. Lily, you've been my best friend since freshman year, and you've been there for me ever since. The good days and bad, the crazy dates and panic sessions. Ben, I'm glad we were in that advanced psychology class together. It was because of that the two of you became the start of my favorite career ever."

Parker leaned over to Ashley as cheers and clapping took over the room. "What career is that?"

"Oh, she owns a matchmaking company."

A matchmaking company? It both intrigued and frightened him. Was she able to make a living at something like that? And the other part of him wanted to stay far away. He didn't need to be pressured into love, especially not by some self-proclaimed professional.

When the applause died down, the girl smiled and continued, "I don't have a whole lot of experience in lasting relationships of my own, but I know Robert Frost had it right when he said, 'Two roads diverged in a wood, and I took the lesser traveled by.' As long as you do it together, life is bound to be one great adventure for the two of you. Congrats, Lily and Ben. I love you both." She raised her glass and nodded.

Parker watched as she smoothed out her dress and sat. As he studied her features, the blond hair swept back, the soft, pointed nose, something broke loose in his chest. And the sincerity of her words caused him to wonder who she was deep down. She'd been so flustered during the procession, he hadn't noticed the full effect of her beauty. But she was well-spoken, and her irritation of him when he'd asked where he was sitting earlier made him want to annoy her even more.

Leaning over to Ashley, he asked, "Do you know much about her business? The matchmaking one, I mean."

With a nod, the girl swallowed the bite of vegetables and patted off her lips with the cloth napkin. "Yes, I've heard a lot of good things and if things don't work out in the next few weeks, I'm ready to sign up."

"What things are you hoping will work out?" Parker sliced through the soft butter, spreading it across his roll.

With a bashful smile, Ashley said, "I kind of like Drew. But please don't tell him. We've hung out a few times, and I'm hoping it turns into something more."

"Take my advice. Just tell him how you feel. Most of the time, guys are oblivious to how a girl feels. The worst that can happen is he'll say he's not interested, and you can move on."

Ashley gulped with an exaggerated motion and nodded, looking as though she'd seen a ghost.

"Wait, didn't she just say in her speech she's not good with her own relationships? How does her matchmaking work, then?"

Ashley's face relaxed, and she leaned in closer, as if her information were top secret. "From what I've heard, she swore off men because she caught her last boyfriend cheating on her, and her mom is some kind of psycho relationship person."

Swore off men? Bart's words from the night before echoed through his mind. This could be good. The seeds of a plan took root in his mind. "What do you mean her mom—"

"She's like a serial dater. She's been married a few times and goes through boyfriends like once a month."

How could he spin that information to help him in the girlfriend department? If she'd sworn off men, he wouldn't have to worry about getting stuck in a long-term relationship. It was the best news he'd heard in the past twenty-four hours. Now he just had to make an offer and seal the deal.

"Thanks, Ashley. You've been a big help."

CHAPTER 7

The speeches ended, the dishes cleared, and they had moved the tables to the sides, allowing room for the first dance between the newlyweds. Meg stood watching Lily and Ben take the floor, most of her excited for the fairytale ending. When she'd met Ben in her psych class senior year of college, she'd had an inkling he might be a good match for her artistic and somewhat dramatic roommate. They'd gone through a lot in the past few years, but this was the start of their life together, and Meg's matchmaker side was beaming. She just wasn't sure how she'd find another roommate quite like Lily.

She glanced around the room and somehow found those clear-blue eyes staring at her. With a jerk of her head, she focused on the bride and groom, rubbing her neck as heat coursed up and into her cheeks. What was her deal? And why did she keep locking eyes with the guy?

As the song came to a close, Drew walked over and bowed before her, taking her hand and pulling her onto the dance floor. They should've practiced more before this, and she held back a curse as he stomped her big toe. Drew had many talents, but dancing wasn't one of them. After pushing back, he fell into step with her lead, and she smiled, as dozens of faces stared at them.

She turned to find Lily dancing with her father, and Ben swinging his mother around the floor. That ache of loneliness turned sour in her mouth, breaking her concentration, and her heel turned. She was able to correct her balance before pulling them both to the ground, but she had to concentrate, even staring at their feet for several beats before looking back up.

By the time the song was over, she left the dance floor, zoning in on the cups of water set on a high table to the side. Grateful to hear the newest Cold Star song being played, she made her way over and got a drink. She had been trained in the more classical dances, and the upbeat tempo of the popular boy band went against all of it.

She stood next to the table, savoring the cool water. Checking her watch, her heart sank. It was only eight o'clock. Her night wouldn't end for two to three hours, between dancing and cleanup. It had already been a long day, and she could use some time away from the constant buzz of conversation. And getting out of these heels would be a relief.

"What are you doing over here?" Lily shouted, cupping a hand behind her ear to hear.

"I needed a drink." Meg raised the cup and took another long gulp, draining the rest of the contents.

Lily reached out her hand and pulled Meg onto the dance floor. So much for missing out on the pop song. They were right in the center, moving around with all the other brides-maids and groomsmen. The heat level soared, and Meg knew it was only time before the smells of sweating bodies hit her. She wasn't used to this mosh pit type of dancing, but she could pretend, at least for one night. It was her best friend's big day after all.

The song ended, and couples paired up, swaying to the first beats of a Frank Sinatra song. Ben nodded to Meg as he took Lily's hand, pulling her close and whispering something in her ear. The smile she gave him was priceless, and hot tears welled up in Meg's eyes. She looked away, trying to get a hold of herself.

What was her deal? She was the one who'd told herself going on a man-free diet would heal and protect her broken heart. And it had been the best for her. She'd been able to find herself again, after all Steve's swipes at her confidence. It hadn't hurt less than any other breakups but Love, Austen wouldn't be where it was without that motivation to make something in her life work out.

Taking a deep breath, she raised her chin, resolved to make it through the night with no tears. She'd smile and chat and get back to her routine tomorrow. It was the best way to protect her heart.

She turned, deciding she'd better leave the middle of the dance floor to stay strong, when she ran right into Mr. Tall, Dark, and Handsome.

"I'm so sorry. I was just—"

He held out his hand, causing Meg to stop short. "Would you care to dance?"

She stared at his hand and then up at his face, her brain struggling to compute the action. Reaching forward, she laid her hand in his, surprised at how small it looked in his large palm. He slid his hand around her waist, causing a heatwave to burst out from his fingertips along her back.

"Would it be all right if I lead now?" He leaned forward to whisper, his breath against her ear sending a shiver down her neck.

"Yes. Sorry. Most guys don't dance well, but I see you've

taken a class or two." She tried to smile at him but when he caught her staring again, she wondered if she looked like a puppy waiting for a bowl of water. The thought sent dread through her. Okay, so she wasn't the best at analogies.

Moments ago, she'd been whining to herself that she had no one. Now, this broad-shouldered man was twirling and sweeping her along the dance floor, and she wondered if she was dreaming.

His hand pulled her a few inches closer, causing the air to hitch in her throat. What was he doing? She glanced away so he wouldn't see the panic in her eyes.

Calling up his name from earlier, she said, "So, Parker Matthews. How do you know the bride and groom?"

"You remembered my name. Well done." His lopsided grin made her stomach flip. "I'm a childhood friend of Ben's. We grew up in the same neighborhood, graduated the same high school. We row together on the weekends now."

"How come I've never heard Ben mention you?" She cocked her head, studying his features. The sharpness of his jaw only added to his features.

"Ben calls me Matt, or Matthews."

The name Matt along with rowing clicked in her brain. "What is it you do, Mr. Matthews?"

"Parker, please. Mr. Matthews was my father, and I'm not that old yet." He chuckled, and the deep sound felt like a shot of electricity in her core. She smiled, trying not to give away too much.

"You still haven't answered my question."

He let go of her hand and pulled at his collar, exaggerating the action. "I didn't realize I'd be interrogated when I asked you to dance."

Shame filled her, and she had to restrain herself from putting her hands to her cheeks, feeling like she'd been sunburned. She dropped her head to the purple paisley tie he wore. Looking back up, the intensity of his eyes struck again. Words poured out.

"I'm sorry. I have to ask a lot of questions for my job, and sometimes I forget to rein it in."

"Do you ask that many questions as a matchmaker?" She missed a step, and he held onto her, getting their feet back in line.

"If I want to be the best matchmaker, yes. Who told you that's what I do?" She was the one who knew everyone, and yet her knowledge on him was next to nothing. The irritation was like a chick pecking at its shell, trying to break free.

That one was bad, even for you, Meg. No more comparisons.

"That you're in the love business? I looked you up when that one lady went on and on with her toast." A chuckle escaped his mouth, and her eyes widened. "Don't worry, I didn't pull crime records. I looked at your website. You said something about not being good with relationships in your speech. What makes you qualified to be a matchmaker, in that case?"

She straightened, her jaw working back and forth. "Not everyone can be great in a relationship, but I have a talent for matching people. I have dozens of clients who are happily matched from my services."

"I'm not judging. It's not like I'm the poster child of happy relationships." He gazed over her shoulder, and she was even more curious about him. Her brain went to work, compiling all the details she knew about him so far. His eyes flicked back to hers and something about the neutral set of his mouth triggered something in her brain.

Meg raised an eyebrow. "Are you the guy the newspapers always claim is the one-date wonder?"

"Ouch."

"I'm sorry, I was just quoting." She felt her mouth go dry as he pulled her another inch closer.

Parker shook his head. "It's kind of true." They moved in silence for a moment before he said, "Divorce lawyer."

"That's your job?" Her eyes flew open as she clicked that detail into its place in her imaginary file of Parker Matthews.

He smiled. "Don't seem so surprised. I thought you read the papers."

She shook her head. "No, I've just seen your picture a few times in magazines my clients read. Sounds like a tough business, especially if you ever wanted a relationship."

"You act like divorce is the worst thing that could happen to someone. What about sickness or death?" The hint of a smile was gone. She'd touched a nerve.

"It is the worst thing. It's like giving up on your dream life."

"Says who?" His eyes narrowed, and Meg froze. Could he see right through her with those things?

Taking a breath, she broke her gaze and focused on his lips. "Says every romantic out there." She didn't sound as confident as she wanted to, her thoughts churning up the idea of how good his lips would feel against hers.

The song ended, and both dropped their hands, snapping the odd daydream that played like a movie through her mind. She hadn't realized how close they'd gotten, and she breathed in cinnamon, the scent tingling her nose and making her head spin.

"Do you want a drink?" He held out his arm to her, and Meg wasn't sure what to do with it. Sure, she'd seen men do this on every romance movie ever. But as she thought over her relationship with Steve, he'd barely held her hand in public, let alone escorted her anywhere.

Sliding her hand through his arm, she said, "Sure. I'm parched."

"Are we in the 1800s? You can't just say you're thirsty?" His lips tried to hide a smile, and she laughed.

"I happen to like the 1800s, thank you very much. Things were a lot simpler back then."

"You're telling me. What would you like?"

"Root beer." His eyebrow raised, and she stuck out her chin. "It's a wedding, not a bar. I take my duties as maid of honor seriously."

He turned and gave their order to the guy behind the bar, grinning when he got the same. She took a drink of the bubbling brown liquid, and it burned all the way down, causing her eyes to water some. She didn't have to tell him she only drank water or lemonade on a normal day.

As soon as she took another sip, his deep voice said, "My boss told me yesterday that if I wanted to be a partner in the firm, I had to find a girlfriend."

Her eyes snapped to his, searching for some joke. Why was he telling her this?

"Really? A divorce law firm requires you to have a significant other? That's like something a comedian would joke about." She chuckled, and he joined in. Was her run of bad analogies coming to an end? She better not chance it with another one.

"That's what I told him. It's not required, but it's 'strongly suggested.' They want to decide in the next few weeks." He took a sip of his drink, and she saw his eyes studying her.

Meg bit her bottom lip, wondering how to respond to that. She set her glass back on the counter and turned to him. The phone call from yesterday rang through her head again.

"I'm in an interesting position now too. I want to get an app created for the business to compete with the bigger companies. I applied for a loan from an investing company a few months back. After an interview with one of their board members, they said I've passed the first test, but they want proof I believe in my process."

"How can they measure that?" Parker's eyebrows cinched together.

"That I'm in a serious relationship. As much as I like the 1800s, it's nice to choose what I want in life. And so far, I'm good at matching myself up with sleaze buckets." She leaned in as she looked around and whispered, "I told the man I have a boyfriend, but I don't."

A strange thrill shot through her. She'd just shared that little secret with a stranger. What if he was from the investment company?

Gulping from the glass in her hand, her nose burned from the carbonation. The silence felt awkward, like she'd shared too much too soon. That was typical for her, but something intrigued her about Parker. Maybe it was the matchmaker in her that wanted to see if she could cure his inability to stay in a relationship longer than a handful of days.

Silence shifted the air between them, and Meg stared out at the dance floor. When she heard his voice again, she turned, studying him. He'd stiffened when she'd called him a one-date wonder. Why would a guy as drop-dead gorgeous as this one not have some supermodel hanging off his every word?

"What if we helped each other out? I've got a history I don't want to repeat when it comes to girls, and it sounds like you've got baggage of your own." He paused, as if trying to decide something. "What if we fake dated?"

"First of all, you don't know me, so don't assume I have baggage. Second, fake date? It's not like I've got to take you to some family gathering for show. This is my business on the line." She hadn't even thought of fake dating. Her first thought was that it would solve all her problems. But then the realization that if anyone ever found out the matchmaker couldn't find her own match, her business would disappear. Had she dropped so low to only date when it wasn't real?

He must have sensed her emotional rollercoaster because he continued, his words coming out faster than pouring milk into a glass. She groaned. *Stop. You're getting worse.*

"Okay, apologies about the baggage comment. But yeah, fake date. I mean we'll share facts about each other, so we know intimate details. Not *too* intimate," he said, raising his hand as she opened her mouth to protest. "But enough so we look like we actually date. Then I'll be there for the events with your investors, and you'll show up to things relating to my partnership. Once we've gotten what we want, we can just tell everyone we broke up."

She bit at her nail, staring at him. Was he serious? From the lack of any upward motion of his lips, he seemed to be.

"What if I say no?"

Parker shrugged his shoulders. "Then we aren't any worse off. But we can help each other, and there are no strings attached. No hurt feelings, and we get what we want."

Her heart beat against her rib cage. It had healed over the last year from Steve's betrayal with his co-worker. It seemed like a surefire way to protect her heart and get the funds she needed to create the app.

"Okay. For the good of my business… I will be your fake girlfriend."

CHAPTER 8

*H*e heard the hesitancy in her voice, but his hope soared. An up-and-coming female business owner, one who could spit fire if necessary. She would put him a leg up in the partnership race, for sure. He pictured Connor's face now, hardened with fury as Parker's fake girlfriend clinched the deal.

"When can you get together to discuss details? Tomorrow?" He didn't want to push her, but they only had a few weeks to pull this off.

"Let me see." She turned away from him, fiddling with her dress. When she turned back around, she had a phone in her hand.

"Where did you hide that with no pockets?" How was that even possible? Her dress hugged all the right curves but... he had to stop there. She'd accepted his offer, and he didn't want to give her enough time to change her mind.

With a raised eyebrow, she ignored him. After scrolling, punching, and squinting, she said, "Tomorrow works. We have a gala every year, and I've got to finalize a lot of details this week."

Parker smiled, amazed he'd been able to find someone to solve his problems this easily. Less than twenty-four hours after Bart told him to find a girlfriend. It took a lot of restraint not to fist pump.

"What time can I pick you up?"

"How about we meet somewhere? There is a little French creperie close to my building, and it serves the most amazing Nutella hot chocolate. Would that work?"

Parker nodded. "Depends on where your building is. My buddies and I row on Saturday mornings. But I could meet around ten."

"It's down Beacon Street. Get off at the Coolidge Corner stop on the C-line. Give me your phone." She reached her hand out and wiggled her fingers, waiting for him to comply.

As beautiful as her manicured fingers looked, he wondered how steady she was with her hands. He'd already seen her lack of grace in heels, and his phone was his lifeline to everything and everywhere he needed to be. Sticking his hand into his jacket pocket, he pulled out the smartphone.

"Wow! This thing is ginormous." Meg turned it over in her hands, looking as though he was carrying an entire laptop around with him.

With a chuckle, Parker said, "Compared to your kid's play phone, I'm sure it looks that way. You break it and you die. Even Karen, my assistant, can't keep up with my schedule on that thing. I'd be lost without it."

Meg swiped a few times and then pushed buttons like those teenagers who amassed thousands of texts sent a month, handing the phone back to him as a sound buzzed from her phone. She tapped away and then said, "Okay, I've got you saved in my phone. Shoot me a text when you're there." Someone called her by name. "That's Lily's mom. Duty calls."

"See you tomorrow," he said, trying to keep his excitement even. He didn't want her changing her mind five minutes after agreeing to the scheme.

She waved and slid off the stool. As she hurried through the crowd, the heels accentuated her calves every step of the way. Those heels were worth it. How he'd found a girl to "date" so soon, he didn't know. And she was beautiful to boot. He could have done much, much worse.

CHAPTER 9

The train stopped, and the doors swung open. Meg was the first one off as she hurried to cross the street, pulling open the door to the creperie as she took off her coat. Boston weather was fickle. Freezing temperatures when she left the house this morning, but now, with the sun out, it felt like spring.

She shrugged out of her coat, draping it over her arm. With a quick pull to the bottom of her blouse, she looked around and saw the top of Parker's head. After a few strides in his direction, she saw his face was only a few inches from the screen of his laptop, one hand covering his mouth in concentration. Dropping her stuff on the empty chair opposite him, she pulled her wallet out of her purse.

"I'm sorry I'm late. Let me get a drink, and I'll be back."

"No need." Parker didn't so much as break his concentration from the laptop as he lifted a small coffee cup from the table and handed it to her. "I remembered you said something about hot chocolate. I hope it's the right one." He glanced up, one eyebrow raised as he watched her take a hesitant sip. She preferred not to have numb taste buds for the next few days.

The warm liquid filled every crack, soothing the irritation she felt at arriving late. The train always took longer when it reached ground level as compared to when it ran beneath the city. This was the second time she'd been late to an appointment this week because of it.

"You didn't have to do that," she said over the cup, sipping at it again. She took the opportunity to stare at him while his attention was distracted. The slight scruff only added to the chiseled features and penetrating eyes. Why wasn't he attached?

The matchmaker part of her brain tried to interfere, wondering in which category he'd fall if he were one of her clients. But he wasn't.

This was a business deal, and she wouldn't get attached.

Shutting his laptop, Parker folded his arms and leaned on the table. "I wanted to do it. Can you imagine standing in that line right now?" He gestured to the line that stretched almost to the door. She'd stood at the very end before, and it would have been awhile.

"And if we're going to be in a," he leaned over and whispered, "fake relationship, we might as well act like it when we're together, right?"

Meg bristled. "Are you saying I couldn't be in a relationship for real? This recent bout of dating celibacy is the result of a cheating jerk and a growing business." Clapping a hand over her mouth, she shut her eyes and shook her head. "Smooth, Meg."

Parker shifted back against the padded booth behind him, his arms held up in surrender. "Whoa, I didn't mean anything by it, and I know how you feel. Sometimes a break can be good. So, do you want to start with the cheating jerk?"

His eyebrow quirked while the other side of his mouth lifted, making him look a little more mischievous.

"Why not?" More resigned than she thought. "He was a former client. A year after I set him up with his matches, he was single. I should've taken that as the first sign something was wrong with him."

She saw Parker's eyes narrow, his pursed lips a sign he didn't believe her. "Is your track record that good?"

Leaning forward, Meg said, "I'm that good. Well, the process is anyway. Obviously, I can't keep track of everyone's lives after they stop coming to me but, usually at least one of the matches works out." She took a big gulp of her hot chocolate, mentally preparing herself for the crash of memories she knew would come.

"We started hanging out. He moved fast, saying I love you within the first couple of months and talking about marriage only weeks after that."

"Did you say it back?"

"What?" Meg went back over her words, trying to figure out what he meant.

Parker ran a hand through his chestnut hair and said, "Did you say, 'I love you?'"

Setting her cup on the table, Meg grabbed a napkin to wipe at the spot she'd dripped on her pants. "Is that pertinent to the state of our relationship? Can I object to the question?"

The sound of Parker's laughter caused her to look up and smile. "Using my job against me. Yes, you can object. I was curious."

"I never told him those three words." She looked up, setting the napkin on the table. The curiosity on his face surprised her.

"You can't even say them out loud." He leaned forward, encroaching on her side of the table. The corners of his lips turned up as he asked, "Have you ever said them to someone?"

Gritting her teeth, she wished she could slide right to the ground and out of the creperie. With such a pointed look, she was sure he could see right through her. "No. I haven't." She paused a moment, staring into his crystal-blue eyes. "What about you, Mr. One-Date Wonder?"

He cringed, but the emotion passed as he shifted his shoulders down. Opening his mouth, it took a few seconds for him to respond. "I've said it once. But we're still talking about you. How did you find out he was cheating on you?"

"I came home early from work to surprise him on his birthday. They were making out on the couch." She studied his face, trying to read his reaction. Was the stoic look on his face his mask for the courtroom? "Not my finest moment, but I've heard they're still together. I guess keying his car wasn't enough of a deterrent." Leaning forward, she tried to paste on a serious expression, but she felt her mouth betraying her. "It's your turn. Who's the girl you proclaimed your love to?"

Sadness passed over his face before he replaced it with the mask. "A girl from law school." He wouldn't look at her, picking at the skin around his thumb. She opened her mouth to say something but clamped it shut when he continued with his gaze still averted.

"I had planned this grand proposal," he said, his eyes glazing with the memory. "After reserving our favorite restaurant and hiring a string quartet, I'd gotten my grand-mother's ring from my father the day before."

The soft spot in Meg's chest was almost mush as she pictured the details. Knowing it ended badly didn't help with the sensation.

"Something tipped her off, and I hurried down on one knee, reaching for the box in my suit coat. She held up her hand and said, 'No. I'm sorry, Parker, but I'm leaving. I'm taking a job in Seattle.'" He raised his gaze but focused on something over Meg's shoulder, the muscle in his jaw tight.

Meg couldn't find the words to respond to that. The fact that he'd put so much effort into the proposal and then such a harsh dismissal, caused her stomach to twist. She hadn't been that far along in her relationship with Steve, but she could relate at least somewhat.

"What did you do?"

He shrugged. "I'm not proud of it, but after three years, I'd spent a lot of time imagining our life together, and she'd just thrown them out the window, without involving me in the decision. I'd always thought those life-changing details were important enough to talk about with someone you loved but apparently, she didn't feel the same." He sipped from his cup. "I stood up, snapped the box closed in her face, and walked away. We haven't spoken since."

Meg smiled. "Well, that's a lot better than hitting things." She giggled, and Parker gave her a close-lipped smile.

"I might have taken out a garbage can driving back to my apartment." His look turned sheepish, and Meg laughed aloud. A snort followed, causing them both to feed off each other.

When they settled down, he asked, "Have you ever been proposed to?"

She savored the hot chocolate a moment as she tried to cover her shock at such a question. They'd known each other all of a few hours, and he was already treading in deeper water than she was comfortable with.

He must have seen her hesitation because he gave her a quick smile. "If it's too personal, you don't have to answer. But those are details people like to bring up to sabotage relationships, especially if they're poking around, say, for an investment."

She hadn't even thought that far into the whole thing. Of course they needed to be prepared for just about anything that the investment board or his firm would ask them.

Shaking her head, she said, "No, I've never gotten that far in a relationship. Besides, to find someone who can put up with me and my schedule, or my mother for that matter, seems to be quite the rare find."

"What do you mean by putting up with your mother?"

Should I share that part of my life? She hadn't seen her mother in at least six months, since she'd moved in with Gerald just outside of Boston. No wonder things had been so calm.

"Long story short, my dad died when I was ten, and it was rough for a few months. We didn't know how to keep going without him there. My mom shut herself in her room and wouldn't come out for days. Thank goodness for Lita, our next-door neighbor. She checked in every night, bringing food and making sure we were all right.

"I remember the night my mom opened the door dressed to go out. We'd buried my dad exactly a month before. She knocked on my door and told me a babysitter was coming by to keep an eye on me for the night. She's been married three more times and has gone through who knows how many boyfriends."

Parker rubbed his eye with a finger, blinking a few times before speaking. "Do you live with her?"

"No. I haven't since I went to college. Why?"

"Well, you said a guy would have to put up with her. I wondered to what extent."

Meg couldn't help but laugh. "Virginia Greyson is a whirlwind. She leaves destruction in her wake every. single. time. Just hope you won't have to meet her in the next few weeks."

"I'm surprised I haven't met her already with how many

times she's been divorced." Parker smiled at her, and Meg tried to smile, the comment hurting more than she cared to admit. As much as she wanted to joke about her mother's dating life, it only made her think of her father, of how things had been with him alive. How would she view her mother if her father were still around?

Tension filled the air around them, and Meg did what she could to release it. "For the record, I like street tacos, people watching, and long walks along the Charles River. Popcorn should always be mixed with chocolate candy, and someday I want to visit Europe. What about you?"

"You sound like you've thought about it. Okay, let me think." Parker tapped his finger against his mouth and raised an eyebrow. She felt a little burst of butterflies take off in her stomach. Was it just the change from the mask he put on? Or was he even more attractive when he thought?

Put on the brakes, Meg. You're just his fake girlfriend. Business contract only.

He looked straight at her, his eyes staring into her own. Grateful she was seated, she moved her legs to make sure they were still connected to her body, because they felt like putty.

"I like a good steak, reading, rowing, and the rush of winning my client the things he or she deserves. Europe is amazing, by the way, and I can't sleep with socks on."

"Seriously? My feet get too cold without them." She loved the laugh that came from deep down in his stomach. "Okay, we should come up with some rules. Are we allowed to tell anyone about our arrangement?"

They sat in silence for a few moments, the bustle of people ordering and finding a seat buzzing around them.

Parker broke the silence. "I say no. The fewer people who know about it, the better. It will help us keep up the act."

"Agreed. I think that's for the best as well." Her thoughts

turned to the wedding the night before. "It's probably good Ben and Lily are gone for the week. She can smell my lies a mile away."

He grinned at her, and she wondered what he was thinking. Staring at his perfect white teeth, she wondered what his ex-girlfriend was thinking. This guy was gorgeous. How did she walk away from him?

Okay, butterflies. Settle down in there. Do you not understand 'fake?' She'd be walking away from him soon enough, and if she were lucky, her heart would still be intact.

"Any other rules?"

Parker shook his head. "We're both adults. Just keep things fun, and we'll play off each other."

Meg nodded and took another sip, gesturing to the laptop in front of him. "What were you working on?"

"I've got a big case coming up. I'm representing Julia Vellardi in her divorce."

With a quick gasp, Meg leaned forward, her eyes probably looking like she was some lunatic. "You mean the Julia Vellardi of the Vellardi wedding line? She's my top recommendation when anyone asks."

"That's the one. It's going to be a rough one. We've had to stop two settlement meetings because of the fighting. It might have to go to court." He picked up his cup and took a long draw, which allowed Meg a moment to mourn. How did someone who created such beautiful dresses and wedding décor end up in a divorce battle? Even though Meg knew a fairytale ending probably wouldn't happen for her, she hoped it would for the rest of the world.

"I bet it's hard to even consider a relationship when you have to deal with people's dirty laundry every day. My hat's off to you."

He snickered, pointing to her. "I don't know how you deal with people in love every day. They can be so annoying."

Meg tossed her head back, thinking of a recent couple. "You're right, but there's a sort of thrill I get from it. Almost like I'm filling my need for love vicariously through them." Meg slipped her large bag over her shoulder and draped her coat over her arm. "I was hoping you'd have time to come look at my office. The process is crazy, and it might be good in case investors ask you any questions when we're together."

He nodded and slipped his laptop into his briefcase. "Sure. Nothing like seeing business from the other side."

When he held the door open for her, she opened her mouth to object, but the look on his face caused her to clamp her mouth shut. It wasn't every day she had an attractive man opening her door. Might as well enjoy it while it lasted.

CHAPTER 10

"*H*ow long have you been here?" Parker asked. He glanced up at the sign on the building, noting the curlicue font of Love, Austen, a daisy taking the place of the 'O.'

Meg grunted as she unlocked the door and pulled it open. "We started with some renovations a couple of months ago, and we've been here about two weeks now."

He walked into what looked like a parlor from his grandmother's house. The pale-blue paint next to the decorative white trim was a bold choice compared to the light-grey walls of his office, but it was bright and cheery.

An old grandfather clock chimed set against a wall. The dark wood of the furniture contrasted with the brightness of the walls, and some of the carvings were so intricate on the armrests, he had to lean forward to make sure his eyes were seeing what he thought he saw.

"Where'd you find this stuff? Isn't there a new furniture store just a few blocks down?" Flames blazed in her eyes, and he held up his hands in defense. "Sorry, I shouldn't have said that."

"It's from the Georgian time period, like the 1800s?" He waited for her to add in, "Duh!" Instead, she folded her arms across her chest and waited for him to nod.

She pointed to the first door on the right. "We use it for storage, for now anyway." She opened the door next to it, the one next to the grandfather clock, revealing two desks on either wall, a computer on each. The room lacked decoration except for a single painting on the opposite wall. The large landscape felt off in such a small room.

"What's this room used for?"

Meg put her hands together, and he could see the excitement sparkling in her eyes, such a different emotion from moments before. Quick mood changes. He'd have to remember that.

"We have each client take a test to give us more information to better match them. How they'll react in certain situations, their favorite things to do, their pet peeves, etc. It helps us in the matching process."

Parker nodded, stepping back to move on with the tour. When she turned to look at him, he knew he was in for it.

"I was thinking," she bit the inside of her lip, drawing his attention to the fullness of both lips, "you should take the test. Then if the investors ask, we can 'show' that we're matched. I can have Tiffany manipulate the results to look like we're compatible, and we'll go from there."

"Sure. If it'll help your cause, I can answer a few questions." Parker stuffed his hands into his pockets, waiting for her to continue the tour.

She nodded and moved past the next door. "That is my office," and then she opened one behind the reception desk. "And this is where I do most of the matchmaking work. Well, I haven't done much in here yet, but I will."

Parker turned to see four big-screen TVs mounted to the wall. Meg moved to a desk with a small monitor on top, and the TVs clicked on. He pulled a chair from the back wall, placing it next to Meg. He sat on it backwards, resting his arms and head on the backrest as he watched her work.

She moved the mouse and clicked on a yellow box on the screen. Her fingers flew over the keys, and it amazed Parker as he saw the accuracy on the monitor. He'd always struggled to type well, and at the rate she was going, she was at least twice as fast.

The first screen flashed pictures of four people, and to the side of each, it summarized their likes and dislikes.

"My tech guy Jorge just finished this program last week. It's an expensive build, but it's already saved me time matching. I look at their picture, see what category they fall into, and get to work figuring out things that will match them with at least three people of the opposite sex."

She switched to another screen, and Parker lifted his head, squinting to read the column headings. Mr. Knightley, Emma, Mr. Darcy, Elizabeth. With ten columns, things clicked into place.

"You use Jane Austen characters to categorize people?" She sat up straight, and her typing turned into a stabbing motion. Parker wanted to reach out and rescue the keyboard.

"Maybe," she said through clenched teeth.

"Well, that explains the old-school furniture then." He ran a hand through his short cut hair and worked to smooth it back down. "And the name of the company."

She smirked at him, her irritation gone. That was fast. "Austen is my last name, and I'm surprised you connected the look of the lobby at all. I don't tell most of the men which category they fall into. They don't understand what the different names are for." With a pause, she pursed her lips before asking, "How do *you* know about Jane Austen?"

"English major. There isn't much I didn't have to read during all those lit classes. I've only read *Pride & Prejudice*, but we talked about a few of the others in class." He glanced at the screen again before turning to her. "I've always thought women who obsessed over her stories were a little desperate. But it looks like you've found one way to use that to your advantage." He leaned back, enjoying the fire in her eyes at his comments.

"Just because you have to work with the jilted doesn't mean you can demean how I earn a living." Her eyes flashed. He'd found at least one button to push.

Giving her a sly smile, he asked, "Are you one of those crazy, 'I'll only fall in love if I find Mr. Darcy' girls?"

She scraped something with her fingernail on the desk, taking a few moments before responding, "No. It's more like I'm waiting for my Mr. Knightley." She turned then, her eyes wide as if she just realized what she'd said. Her words sped up as she stumbled over them. "The only people who know are Lily and Tiffany. Just… just don't tell anyone that, okay?"

Parker made a face. "Mr. Knightley? Like the guy who could've been Emma's father?"

"Okay, he wasn't that old. He's a good friend and isn't afraid to tell her his mind. Granted, she doesn't listen to it until she realizes she loves him, but they don't seem that far apart in age."

"How old are you, if I might ask?" If he had to guess, he would say twenty-four.

"Twenty-six. And you?"

"I turn thirty at the end of the month. So, if you're Emma, I guess I won't be ringing up as Mr. Knightley on your test." He grinned as she scrunched her nose at him, hitting his shoulder with the back of her hand.

"Please. That's not the only indicator of the category you're in. The test takes in everything. Why don't we have you do that now?" She stood, waving her hand as if she were trying to get some unwanted animal out of the room.

Parker stood and placed the chair back against the wall. "Are we done with the tour already?"

"We have two more floors. The second floor is our studio with a dance floor and a wall of mirrors. We do a lot of the group classes and workshops up there. The third floor will be a salon one day, when I get the funds to finish it. We offer makeovers for things like the gala coming up, and it will be nice to have it in-house one day."

"I take it I'll be attending the gala?" He held his breath, hoping she'd tell him no.

She gave him a side look and nodded. "It's in three weeks, and the investors will be there."

They made it to the door where the computers sat, and Parker swung towards her, catching her off guard. "Why were you defensive when I asked about how you categorize your clients?"

She stiffened again. "Because most people think I live in a fantasy world when I tell them that, just like you accused me of. They don't take my business as seriously, when I've done a lot of work to synthesize her works and human character-istics to matchable traits."

With a nod, Parker said, "It sounds like you've found success with it. Why are you ashamed?"

"Just another side effect from the cheating boyfriend, I guess." She smiled, her lips closed. "Let me know if you need anything. Good luck on your test." She turned to walk back to the other room, and Parker watched her go, surprised he couldn't pull his eyes away. Her jeans hugged her hips just right, and she moved with more confidence in the pink sneakers instead of the heels.

Fake girlfriend. Don't get attached.

Shaking his head, he sat behind a computer and typed in his name and email.

The test took over an hour to finish and by the end, his

brain was mush. All the questions about favorites and hobbies and past situations blended together. The what-would-you-dos took much longer to answer than they should have. Clicking done, he stood and stretched, yawning as he walked out into the lobby.

When he found no one, he heard a scraping from the back room. Pushing the door open, he saw Meg stretching on top of a small ladder, trying to shove a box onto a shelf in the closet.

With her blond hair thrown up in a ponytail, he could see the curve of her neck. The simple t-shirt and jeans contrasted the dress from the night before, but she looked comfortable and more attractive. Courtney popped into his mind. Had she ever worn anything besides designer suits and dresses?

"So, have you found any Mr. Knightleys in your client pool?" His voice startled her, and she dropped to her heels and swung around, the unbalanced box falling against her in the process. In what seemed like slow motion, her balance shifted backward, and her arms flailed in the air.

His body reacted, lunging forward as he noticed the space between the ladder and the desk was too narrow, hoping to catch her in time. Arriving too late to catch her by the waist, he caught her head in his arms, inches from striking the corner of the desk.

Her eyes went wide, the color of the sea searching his face for something. She choked out, "Thank you," before moving to stand. The smell of orange blossoms hit his nose. With effort, he managed to stay firmly planted. The smell was deli-cious, and it made him lightheaded.

He shrugged. "You keep making me look like a hero. I guess it's right place, right time." He looked at the flush creeping up her cheeks.

She rolled her eyes at him, and a soft smile formed on her

lips. Turning to pick up the box, she shoved the papers back inside, her chest heaving. She'd probably gotten a good shot of adrenaline after that fall. He took it from her, settling it on the shelf without the need of a ladder.

"Of all the characters, I think I relate most to Emma." She kept her eyes on the paperwork.

"Have you not taken your own test?" Parker frowned at her, folding his arms like a stubborn toddler when asked to clean up the toys.

"I took it back in college, but I didn't have all the categories assigned at the time. I haven't had time to retake it with all the updated questions." Her hands twisted together, nervous. She asked, "Did you finish yours?"

Parker stared at her smooth lips, and he wondered what it would be like to kiss them. This woman seemed more complicated than most he'd come across, but there was a magnetism there that kept pulling her toward him. When she said his name, he snapped back to the present.

"Nothing. Sorry? My test. Yes. It should be in your email." Feeling heat rush up his neck, he knew that was his cue to leave. "Call me later and let me know how I did. I'm curious to see which character I am."

She flicked a pen at him across the room, and he laughed, ducking behind the doorframe. He called out, "Bye!" as he pushed the front door open.

Pulling open the door to his car, he wondered why such a woman was still single. Sure, she had her quirks, but didn't everyone else?

CHAPTER 11

Onday dawned, and Meg wished she could curl up into a ball and sleep until the nightmare had passed. Her office chair would only be good for so long, sleep-wise, until she got a crick in her neck. The caterer had emailed, yes, *emailed* her to say they had been double-booked, and they regretted they couldn't keep their commitment to the Love, Austen gala.

They regretted it so much they couldn't even call her. She'd need to get the deposit back pronto. Without it, the attendees would be eating peanut butter and jam sandwiches with the mini packs of cookies from the store.

Juice boxes would be a nice touch to that.

Tiffany walked in with a small piece of paper, her lips rolled in with worry. "I just got off the phone. Most of the décor we ordered is now on back order, and nothing will get here until two weeks after the gala."

Slumping down in her chair, Meg rested her arm over her forehead, wishing she could stop the tidal wave of mistakes from happening. "What are we going to do?"

"I can start looking at other options."

Puffing out her cheeks and then blowing out the air, Meg dropped her arm and stooped forward. "All right. Send me pictures before you order anything. We have to make this perfect if we want our investors to be pleased."

"Did you happen to find a boyfriend along the way?" Tiffany's voice hinted with curiosity. With the wedding and the little interview session yesterday, Meg had forgotten Tiffany didn't know yet.

"I did, actually. He's my fa—I mean, he's my favorite one so far." Meg giggled at how ridiculous it sounded.

Tiffany jutted out her hip, setting her hand on it. "Slow down. When I left here Friday, you were still single. How did you meet someone, go on a couple of dates, and declare yourselves together in two days?"

"Well, I met him at Lily's wedding." Meg searched her brain for details she could use. They say stick as close to the truth as possible, right? "He asked me to dance, and I didn't have to lead for once. Bonus points there." Pulling out a pad of paper, she wrote down the couple of things she needed to grab at the grocery store on her way home. If anything, it helped keep her mind from all the stress adding up that morning.

"That's vague. You've given me better descriptions of clients. What does he look like? What does he do for a living?" Tiffany took a seat across from Meg's desk, the disbelief written all over her face.

Meg indulged in the memories she had of him so far. "His eyes are a light blue, but they work well with his clean-cut brown hair. Strong jaw, and strong arms." She almost sighed as she recalled the two times she'd fallen. It probably pulled her off the list to have a real relationship with him, but he didn't want a girlfriend as much as she didn't want a boyfriend, right?

A few snaps from Tiffany brought her back to the

present. "Are you all right? I've never seen this side of you before."

With a wave of her hand, Meg said, "It's lack of sleep from worrying about this gala. I was just trying to think of what we could do if no other caterer could do it on such short notice." Tiffany nodded in agreement. Poker face. Maybe she'd gotten better at lying.

"What's your *boyfriend's* name again?" Tiffany stressed the word, slurring it, which made Meg laugh. Couldn't she just let it go?

"Parker Matthews. He's a divorce lawyer for some company his dad owned."

Tiffany moved forward, placing her palm on Meg's forehead. "Are you sure you're all right? I've known you almost two years, and this is the first you've talked gibberish."

"I know, I know, not the kind of person a matchmaker should date but if we make it through the month, it will be longer than your boyfriend before Grant."

"Grant was an idiot. Gah, I'm glad that's over. Just like when you finally realized what a jerk Steve was." Meg sat back, a little stunned by Tiffany's reaction. Throughout her time dating Steve, Meg had leaned on Lily for help. It made her feel good she had another friend to be there for her, especially now that Lily had other things to worry about.

"When do I get to meet him?" Her assistant raised both eyebrows as she leaned over on the desk. "Maybe we can get a picture of him to fill this frame. I can't believe you still haven't changed this. I gave it to you months ago."

Pulling the silver frame towards her, Meg said, "And I'm grateful for it. I make up stories about this couple. It keeps things interesting. Besides, who has time to print out pictures these days?" Tiffany wasn't convinced.

"All you have to do is say, 'Tiffany, will you print off a picture of my new love for my picture frame.' There's a CVS down the street. I can take your phone now and get one printed." They'd been working together for too long.

Meg snorted. "We can worry about the frame when we have decorations and a caterer figured out. Help me dig myself out of this hole." Tiffany gave her a look that said she'd be watching from the other room and turned to leave.

"You better let me meet him! I'm still not sure he's real."

"He's real all right," she said under her breath.

Seconds later, Meg's cell phone rang. Parker's name came up, and excitement bubbled up in her stomach, catching her off guard. She paused a moment, trying to keep her voice nonchalant.

"Hey, Parker."

"Hey yourself. How's your morning going?"

"Not too bad," she lied. "Just putting out small fires right now."

He paused on the other line. "So... um... are you free Wednesday evening?"

"I think so. What's up?"

Another pause. "I may have told my boss about you, and now he's invited the three candidates and their significant others over for dinner. I know it's in the middle of the week, but it might be nice to get that first meeting out of the way."

She wanted to laugh at the nervousness in his voice, but she kept it to herself. "You act like I'll say no. Do I need to wear a dress?"

"Hmmm. That's a great question." She could hear the relief in his voice. "What would you normally wear to a dinner party?"

"Probably a dress."

A nervous laugh came through the phone. "Okay, wear one of those. I'll pick you up at seven?"

A moment of panic seized her. A divorce lawyer who came from money probably didn't rent a single room in a house full of renters. Besides, she would still be at the office. Checking her calendar, she was right.

"Just pick me up at my office. I've got a meeting that ends about six-thirty, so we'll go from here." Pulling out a pad of paper, she wrote a reminder to bring the dress and heels to work on Wednesday.

"Sounds great." He was silent again before saying, "Hey, Meg? Thanks again."

She couldn't help but laugh. "No worries. I know the stakes. I will do everything I can to make you look good." When they said goodbye, Meg stared at her phone in her hand. It surprised her that such a confident man like Parker Matthews would be so nervous to ask her out on a fake date. Maybe she'd overestimated him.

CHAPTER 12

*H*e lucked out as he pulled up to the curb next to Meg's office. Finding a spot to park along Beacon or one of the busier streets in Boston was always a toss-up. And to find one directly outside his destination? That never happened.

Checking the clock on the dash, he was six minutes early. Should he go see if she was ready? Or should he wait out here until a few minutes after seven? It had been too long since he'd even worried about dating protocol, and it seemed like he had to push back cobwebs as he tried to remember.

A nervous energy ran through him, something he hadn't felt since the first few dates with Courtney. Sure, he'd gone out with girls since their breakup, but those were for work events, and he usually just found someone to go with him. No attachments and no second dates. Which was why the media dubbed him the "One-date Wonder." He shouldn't complain because that sounded much better than a playboy or a host of other names they could've used.

After dredging up the memory of his failed proposal for Meg, he hadn't been able to rid his mind of Courtney's face from the last time he'd seen her. With raised eyebrows and red lips, she'd looked amazing when she first walked in that night over three years ago. He'd avoided girls who wore red lipstick for at least six months after.

No one should have to be rejected when he, or she, was proposing. He had just been too blind to see the signs.

The weird part about it was that at the end of every bit of that memory, Meg's face replaced Courtney's. The girls were different, in style, attitude, but their drive to succeed was the same. But was Meg the type to leave?

We're fake dating.

When she left, it would be because their agreement was complete. Tapping on his steering wheel, he tried to focus on the words of the latest Cold Star single. At three minutes to seven, Parker turned off the car and got out.

The keys swung back and forth in his hands as he walked up to the door and pulled. Locked. He cupped his hands around his eyes to look through the glass and found everything dark.

Did she forget he was picking her up there? He balled his hand into a fist and knocked on the window a few times. He could feel his heart thunder inside his chest. One thing he didn't appreciate was being made out to be a fool. He pulled his phone out of his suit coat pocket, searching for her name in his contacts.

His mind wandered as he listened to the ringtone. When he told Bart he had found a girl to date, the elation and emotion in the other man's face was as a father for his son. It was the first time he'd realized their relationship was more than a boss and employee. It made him wonder if his own father would have felt the same.

Shoving his hands in his pockets, Parker took in a deep breath filled with train exhaust as it started back up from the stop a few feet away. He walked around, trying to keep himself occupied. She wouldn't have stood him up, would she?

A jiggle of the handle sounded in his ears as he turned to see the door open, and a girl walked out, a smile on her face. She gave him a look and then asked, "Are you Parker?"

He looked around, making sure she was asking him, and said, "Yes. Do you work here? I came to pick her up, but everything was dark inside."

She giggled and stuck out her hand. "Yes, I'm Tiffany. Meg just had to grab something and she'll be out." With an up-and-down glance, the girl smirked. "It's nice to see you're actually real."

"Why's that?"

"I'm just surprised you got her to get serious so fast. She's been—"

The door opened, and Meg said, "Tiffany, what are you doing?" She gave the girl a pointed look, but Tiffany just smiled.

She wore a knee-length black rain jacket and black glittery heels. Her hair was pulled back halfway, the rest of it falling in curls down her back, looking so soft he wanted to touch them. It seemed like some magnetic connection wouldn't let him pull his eyes from her, until she caught him looking.

"I'm meeting your boyfriend, of course. Have you kissed yet?" Tiffany looked between the two of them with a look that said she was pleased with herself for something. Probably the nervous tension now radiating out from Meg.

The question caught Parker off guard, but he smiled wide when Meg said, "A lady never tells."

"So, you haven't. I'm sorry, Meg, but I still don't buy it." Tiffany's hand waved in Parker's direction and then to her boss.

"Oh, shush!" The look of embarrassment on Meg's face

sent him whirling. He walked the few steps towards her, sliding his hand around her neck and pulled her lips to his. Their soft touch against his own caused that tingling feeling after he'd done leg day at the gym.

When her arms wrapped around his neck, he nudged her lips open, deepening the kiss. Fireworks exploded in his chest, and he almost forgot they were on a sidewalk in front of Meg's office.

A loud cough came from Tiffany. "Okay, okay. That's enough. You kids have a good night, and I'll see you in the morning," she said, looking to Meg with a wink. Turning to him, she said, "Nice to meet you, boyfriend. I hope you'll stay longer than a month."

Still recovering from the kiss, the air flew out as if someone had punched him in the gut. Their agreement was only a month but after that kiss, he wasn't sure he could kiss another girl ever again without comparing it to the taste of her lips.

He pointed to the car, and they walked toward it. "Good save. She was drilling me yesterday about it not being possible that we could be a couple so quickly." He could tell she was avoiding looking at him.

Parker opened his mouth but found himself at a loss for words. His lips still tingled, and he wasn't sure how to respond to her comment with his mind buzzing about it.

"Have you been waiting out here long?" Her eyes shone under the streetlight, and he was tempted to call Tiffany back, so he had an excuse to kiss her again.

He shook his head. "No, just a couple of minutes. It was all dark in your office. I thought you'd forgotten."

As he opened the door for her, she smiled. "Thank you." She slipped inside and when he slid into his seat, she said, "I hadn't forgotten. I was getting ready upstairs. There's not much room in the bathroom on the main level."

He turned on the ignition, and glanced over at her. "Are you ready for this?"

"As ready as I will be, I guess. How are you feeling?" Her smile wasn't big, but there was hope behind it.

With a snort, his mind called up the insecurities he'd just played out while waiting for her. "Honestly? I feel like I'm on a constant emotional rollercoaster." That kiss didn't help matters either. His lips felt like embers burning.

She covered his hand with hers as it sat on the shifter. "I know what you mean. We'll get through this together." He felt a chill when she removed it, part of him wishing she'd keep it there. He had felt nothing like this the night of Ben's wedding. What was going on with him? He'd have to get a grip before she left him like a banana peel and split. He chuckled at that thought.

"What's so funny?" Meg looked at him, suspicion on her face.

His brain rushed for words to answer her. "Sometimes the analogies I think are funny, aren't funny to other people."

"I'm the worst at analogies. I told Lily that she and Ben were like ice and water."

Parker bit his lip, trying not to laugh. "What did she say?"

Meg shook her head, sighing with her hand over her eyes. "Something about them being cold. I tried to make it sound better, but then a woman pulled me into place for the procession to start."

"At least we know you have one flaw." Now, he couldn't think of many others. Beside the part about her lack of gracefulness when she was around him, but he liked feeling like her hero.

And yet when they'd danced, she'd matched him step for step without a problem.

"How did you learn to dance?" he asked. As he breathed in, the smell of oranges from her perfume reminded him of their closeness at the wedding, and it caused his whole body to relax.

Biting her upper lip, Meg's eyes went wide, and her smile became forced. "I, uh, well, my mother insisted I be in beauty pageants as a kid. I can be a little clumsy, as you've witnessed." She looked at him out of the corner of her eye and then turned her focus to the road ahead. "She hoped to correct that by having me take just about every dance class within the city limits. Dancing is about the only time I don't have to worry about falling."

"So, you haven't been falling for me then?" He meant it as a joke, but he saw her back tense and turned to focus on not hitting the car in front of them. "I'm just teasing because of the two times… yeah." *Just let it go.*

Meg turned and gave him a small smile. "Don't worry. I get it."

Something about his comment had hit home, pushing another button. But this time, he was sorry he'd done it.

CHAPTER 13

A weird silence settled over the car, and Parker was grateful when they pulled up to Bart's building. A man pulled a cone away, revealing a spot for him along the curb. Leave it to Bart to think of everything, even parking for his guests.

"Thank you, Henry. Is everyone inside?"

"Yes, sir. Go on up."

He held out his hand for Meg, and she took it, stepping out of the car while avoiding his eyes. Was she bugged about his joke?

She stumbled, holding onto him with both arms. As soon as she righted herself, she let go, looking down, and tucked a loose piece of hair behind her ear.

"You can hold onto me. I promise I don't have cooties." A thrill went through him as she slipped her arm through his. She gave him a half-smile, giving him the push to say, "I hope I didn't offend you already. I meant the falling comment as a joke." She visibly relaxed at his words.

"I know, I just feel out of sorts today. Trying to get everything figured out for this gala is a bigger headache than I thought it would be." They walked a few steps, and she turned to him. "You don't know any caterers available two weeks from Saturday, do you?"

"Let me think about it. Heather always has someone on hand for dinner parties. I'd just have to see how many they're willing to serve. How many are you expecting?"

They arrived at the front doors, and he punched in the code. A buzz sounded, followed by a click from the door. He opened it and motioned for her to step through, following close behind.

"Between four hundred and five hundred. Wait, your boss lives here?" Parker only nodded as they walked onto the elevator. He pushed the button for the penthouse.

"He lives in the penthouse? No wonder divorces cost so much." She said it so matter of fact, but the tone in her voice dislodged a chuckle from Parker. "What? What did I say?"

"Nothing. We hear that a lot, more by people who've never been through a divorce than those who've gone through one. But, we put up with quite a lot when dealing with people's issues."

A smirk tugged at her lips, and he waited for her to say something.

"What?"

She laughed. "I was just thinking about the poor lawyer my mom keeps hiring for her divorces. He definitely deserves every penny he earns after putting up with her."

The elevator moved quickly and jerked to a stop, as the doors swung open into the foyer of the home. Parker had been there many times throughout the ten years Bart and his wife, Cherice, had owned it. But that didn't stop him from admiring Meg's reaction to the large open room and expensive decor. Her eyes shot to the windows illuminated by the final rays of sunset. A good chunk of the surrounding parts of Boston sat just outside, giving them a bird's-eye view of it all.

"What do you think?" he asked Meg.

She turned to him, eyes wide. "What do I think? It's incredible. The herringbone floors, the floor-to-ceiling windows, the light fixtures. It's all breathtaking."

He cocked his head and narrowed his eyes at her. "But I thought you were into the older stuff."

"It doesn't mean I can't appreciate good taste in modern decor." She smiled at him, and their eyes locked for a few seconds. He could get lost in the sea of her eyes, the thought releasing tension he'd felt at the thought of getting through the night.

As he reached for her jacket, she whispered, "Is there anything I need to know about tonight? Anyone to stay away from, or I need to make an effort to talk to?"

"If you can connect to Bart's wife, you'll earn some serious brownie points."

"Brownies are good. Especially with ice cream." Meg's eyes twinkled, and he was glad to see that whatever apprehension she'd been feeling, had passed. This side of her was even more attractive. Even when she was off, she was attractive. But he needed to focus on tonight, especially if they were going to convince people they were a couple.

With her coat removed, he saw the black dress, hugging every curve that mattered. With her hair half-down, he felt like he'd won the fake-girlfriend lottery, if there was such a thing. A pull tugged him towards her, and he took a step closer, his gaze dropping to her lips.

"You look amazing." His voice was airy as he said it, causing her cheeks to turn rosy. She looked away, twirling a piece of hair around her finger.

Feeling a clap on his shoulder, Parker broke his gaze away to find Bart standing in front of them.

"Ah, Parker, I'm so glad you could make it. And this must be Miss Austen." He dropped Parker's hand and reached out to shake Meg's. She shook it firmly, her gaze direct and a warm smile on her face. Bart looked impressed as he glanced over to Parker, with a knowing expression.

"You have a firm handshake. I admire that." His boss stuck his hands into his pants pockets, looking even more relaxed in his own home than Parker had seen him in a long time. He'd have to ask him later what had changed.

Meg smiled. "You can tell a lot about a person by their handshake. I like to make an impression."

Bart laughed. "That's true. Parker tells me you two have been hanging out. You're a brave woman to take on a guy with such a big ego." He reached out and landed a soft punch to Parker's chest.

"Now, now. Let's not question the lady's remarkable judgment." Parker chuckled, and Meg shook her head.

Ignoring him, Bart turned back to Meg. "It's a pleasure to meet you, Miss Austen."

"Please, call me Meg."

"All right, Meg. What can I get you to drink?" Parker leaned toward her as he heard a soft hum from her mouth. Did she always do that when she made a decision?

Parker saw her cheek turn a shade of rose, and she batted her eyes a few times before saying, "Lemonade?"

"Coming right up." Bart turned towards the kitchen, waving for them to move into the dining room.

"Don't worry about me, I guess. I'll just stand here, parched," Parker called out, chuckling as his boss ignored him. He saw Meg's head swing to his, and he winked at her. She lifted her hand to hide her laughter, but it escaped, turning heads of the others they approached in the room.

She leaned in. "I can't believe you remembered 'parched.' Best line of the night."

As she took a few steps into the room, he watched her walk to join the group. He felt an invisible string tethering himself to her, and a part of him didn't want to get rid of it.

CHAPTER 14

The setting was intimate, but the table fit the eight guests and their hosts comfortably. The lavender table runner, with its flower design, offset the rest of the white tablecloth. Positioned every so often along the table were clear glasses with floating white candles, and the simple purple design on the china tied it all together.

Meg could feel Parker's nerves fully charged next to her and as she looked down at his hands in his lap, she found him twisting his napkin so tight, she looked for tears in the cloth.

"Are you always this anxious when you come here?" She'd leaned closer to him, not wanting to draw attention to his nerves. The smell of his woodsy cologne drew her in further, causing her eyes to dip to his lips again.

All awareness of what was going on around the table vanished as she replayed their kiss in her mind. How he'd made every nerve in her body hum had thrown her off guard. She'd never felt like that with another guy, least of all Steve. Once this fake relationship was over, she was sure she'd be ruined from kissing anyone ever again.

Parker glanced at her, puzzled, following her eyes to his hands. He released the napkin and tried to fake a smile.

With a slight shake of the head, he leaned in and said, "No. I get nervous before a big court case, but this is like a second home to me."

She rested her hand on top of his, cupping her fingers over the side, hoping to infuse some comfort to him. Moving her thumb over the back of his hand, she saw the sides of his mouth turn up. A jolt of electricity shot up her arm, and she glanced at him, wondering if he felt it as well.

Bart spoke from the end of the table, and Meg turned with her hand still in his, not wanting to let go of the connection they had. At least an audience was a good excuse to keep it there.

"We're honored to have you all here tonight as candidates for a partnership, as well as being good friends and great employees. We're only missing the wife of the late Jeffrey Matthews. Heather flew to be with her mother for hip surgery, otherwise she would have accompanied us this evening." Meg turned to look at Parker, but he seemed focused on Bart.

As she searched her memory for any mention of his mother, Meg realized she'd gone and on and on about her own mother but hadn't asked about his parents. Was the partnership opening because his father died? No wonder her relationships never lasted long. She didn't stop to ask the basic questions about the person.

Two servers came from the kitchen, placing salad in front of each guest.

"We'd love for each of you who came with the candidates to introduce yourself. A partnership is a big responsibility and you, as the significant other, are as important as the ones in the running." Bart picked up the napkin beside his plate and spread it out on his lap. He then looked around the table, waiting for a response to his request.

That was something she hadn't heard before, that a spouse or significant other mattered just as much as the employee. It would be nice to apply it to her own company. But now, her only full-time employee was a college sophomore who didn't date consecutively. As the CEO of the company, Meg was beginning to realize what she'd been missing in the boyfriend department.

Parker squeezed her hand, the corner of his mouth lifting as he glanced at her and then to the other end of the table.

Stop. Don't analyze. You're here to listen and make polite conversation.

Bart pointed to a girl to his left. "Hello. I'm Samantha Caruthers. I'm twenty-two and in my senior year of college at Salem State. I'm a communications major hoping to break into acting soon. Connor and I met several months ago at a charity fundraiser, and we've been together ever since." The girl smiled and while she was pretty, her tone of voice was so high, Meg looked around for a misplaced helium balloon. Connor beamed next to her, looking in Parker's direction. He must be the competition.

Sharon's husband Stanley went next. "I'm a car salesman in Watertown. I love to golf and fish. Sharon and I met twenty years ago—"

"Twenty-three," Sharon mumbled.

"That's right. Twenty-three years ago, at a drive-in movie. We've been married for twenty-one years." He turned to his wife to make sure that number was correct. When she nodded, he breathed a sigh of relief, sending a chuckle down the table. Sharon didn't even crack a smile. Tough crowd, or in Stanley's case, tough life.

Suddenly, all eyes were on Meg, and she smiled, hoping there was nothing in her teeth.

"Hello, everyone. I'm Meg Austen, owner of the matchmaking company, Love, Austen. I've been doing this for about five years now, but we just remodeled a place over on Beacon Street for our new office. I love changing people's lives. Parker and I met at a mutual friends' wedding just a few days ago. Hopefully, we can last as long as Sharon and Stanley over there." Meg pointed to them and clapped, the others joining in. "That's amazing, you two. Congrats."

Cherice's voice sounded from Meg's right, and she turned to listen. "How did you get started in the matchmaking business?"

Bart's chuckle from across the other way made Meg feel like a bobble-head doll. "Watch out. Cherice was a journalist."

Meg smiled, hoping she looked more confident than she felt. "It actually started out as a final project for my psychology class in college."

"Really? And you've been able to make it come to life. That's the start of a great story." Cherice wagged her finger at Meg and smiled.

"Thank you." It sounded weak even to Meg's ears. Another conversation built steam towards the other end of the table, and Meg looked to Parker.

He leaned over to say something, and a wave of his cologne hit her, stronger than before. It made her think of fall afternoons and pine trees.

"I had no idea that's how your business started. Did you get an A?" He'd relaxed some, the hint of teasing in his expression.

Meg nodded. "Of course. My professor was a tool and before I started the project, he told me I'd probably fail the class if I pursued my idea. With all the research I'd done and the profiles I'd created, he couldn't justify failing me."

Resting her back against the seat, she could see her words impressed him, a stupid grin growing bigger as he gazed in

Connor's direction. After a minute or two, he said, "You're doing amazing. It seems Cherice has taken a liking to you. She's a tough one to please, let me tell you."

Meg snuck a glance at the woman now talking to the other partner's wife. "Have you known her that long?"

"Pretty much my whole life. When my mom left, she took on a mom-aunt type of role, and she's always been a good one at giving advice."

Leaning in closer, Meg tried to dismiss the tingles across her shoulders and down her neck from his scent. She spoke even softer. "Your mother left? Her name's not Heather?" She turned to him and saw a moment of sadness pass over his eyes.

He wiped off his mouth with the napkin and set it back down on his lap. "Heather is my stepmother. She and my father married about a year after my mother ran off with her physical trainer."

Puzzle pieces clicked into place as she saw the vulnerability behind Parker's eyes. His mother had left, then his ex-girlfriend when he'd proposed. No wonder he needed a fake girlfriend for this process. Meg placed her hand on his arm and gave it a little squeeze.

One piece of information brought them even closer together. Too bad it was their shared bad luck in love.

"I'm so sorry. I should have asked more about your family."

He shrugged and gave a self-deprecating smile. "The stories about your mom made my family sound tame." His smirk caused her to laugh louder than she had intended. The room went silent as all eyes turned to her.

"I'm sorry. We were just talking about..."

"About that time I got knocked out in court. Do you remember that, Bart?" Relief flooded Meg as Parker gave her a quick wink before turning his attention back to the head of the table. It was her job to make him look good and here he was saving the day.

"How could I forget it? It was your very first case, and I think it was pro-bono, right?" Bart looked to Parker, and he nodded. "You'd tried to plead a case, but your client ruined it all and then slugged you for losing it for her."

Several of the guests laughed at the story, but Meg noticed Connor's mouth down-turned and his jaw working overtime. Nothing like a good competition to keep things interesting.

"Hey, thanks for coming tonight." Parker gave her a half smile before turning back to the road.

"No problem. It helped solidify some things you talked about and hopefully I made a good impression on them." She could feel her stomach tighten as they neared her home. The small, plain bedroom at the top of the creaking stairs would look plain compared to the grandeur of the penthouse.

"I've never seen Cherice so open when she's just met someone, so I would chalk that up to a good night."

Hoping to keep her mind off the growing anxiety at him seeing where she lived, Meg pulled out her phone, checking an email, and then turned to look at him. "Any other meetings I need to put on my calendar?"

"I can't think of any now but as soon as I remember, I'll let you know. Where do I need to turn again?" He leaned forward to turn down the song on the radio a few notches.

She lifted her finger and pointed to the left, her hand just above his arm. "You can drop me off right here on the corner, if you want."

Turning the car, he shook his head, wrinkling his nose in her direction. "It's eleven-thirty p.m. Besides, you just made things easier at my job. If I were one to gloat, I'd say we won this round. Even though we're fake dating, I want to make sure you make it all the way home, not just a block away."

Closing her eyes, she leaned back into the chair. "I know, but I don't live in a penthouse."

"I don't either."

Surprised by this revelation, Meg popped her eyes open and stared at him. "You don't?"

He chuckled. "Did you think everyone in my firm lives in a penthouse?"

Pursing her lips together, Meg frowned. "I guess I hadn't really thought about it." She pointed straight and then asked, "Where do you live?"

"I have an apartment in Beacon Hill. It's small but for the time I'm there, it works."

Even in the darkness, Meg could see the silhouette of the older white house.

"It's that house on the right. The one with the white picket fence out front."

He parked along the curb and unbuckled his seatbelt.

"You don't have to walk me up. I'm just going to run inside and jump in bed. I'm beat."

"Are you sure?" he asked, leaning over his steering wheel to look at the house.

Meg nodded, putting her hand on the handle. "Thank you so much for tonight. It was fun to have a nice dinner for a change. I've been eating a lot of takeout lately with all the craziness at work."

Parker didn't seem to hear her. "Have you lived here long?"

She nodded, biting her lips. If only there was some way to

keep him from investigating the house some more. "Lily and I moved in sophomore year of college, so I've been here about six years now. Since the business moved into the office, it feels like I only come here to sleep. But the rent is cheap, which can be hard to find in Boston. And we've taken care of our landlord over the years. He's like a surrogate father." A lump formed in her throat, and she pushed it down, determined not to leave him with a mental picture of her ugly-cry face.

"Is he all right?"

With a nod, she said, "Yeah, he had a stroke a few years ago. It was scary at the time, but he does really well now." She pulled on the handle. "I better let you go. Didn't you say you have to be in court early tomorrow?"

"Yeah, unfortunately I do. But this was fun. Let me know when I can return the favor." She stared at his even, white teeth, her eyes looking up at his eyes and back down to his lips. Her mind flashed a replay of their kiss earlier, and she wouldn't mind one for dessert.

What am I doing? He doesn't think of me like that. There's no one around to force us to pretend.

Her hesitation and thoughts made her forget he'd said anything. "Sure, yeah. I'll let you know when I look at the calendar tomorrow." She tried to keep her eyes on his, but she kept glancing down at his lips, a heat spreading through her chest.

He leaned in, his lips getting closer. Her lips buzzed, as if preparing for the firework show about to begin. At the last second, his head turned. She felt his arms circle around her, and her stomach sank, disappointed. Returning the hug, she gave him a little pat on the back.

Nothing like putting her in her place.

"Good night." She pushed the door open all the way and waved as she shut it. Not daring to look back, she walked into the house and shut the door, waiting until he drove away.

A strange mixture of relief and sadness flooded her.

Fake boyfriend. Fake boyfriend.

Her heart wasn't convinced, but a girl had to try.

CHAPTER 16

"How did everything go last night?" Tiffany appeared in the doorway of Meg's office, pulling her long hair back into a ponytail.

Meg paused for a second, wondering what to tell her assistant. Not that she hadn't spent most of the night replaying many of the conversations and events.

And the kiss.

"It was a good night. We had dinner in this amazing penthouse right by the Common. The food was delicious. Parker's boss and his wife are fun, and it was good to get to know people he works with."

Tiffany grinned. "So, how was it when he dropped you off?"

"Seriously, Tiff. I feared him seeing my paint-peeling, humble abode. But it was dark so that helped things."

"First of all, if he likes you, he's probably not going to worry about where you live. But can we talk about that kiss? Because I'm sure it was perfect. Well, from an onlooker's perspective." Meg thought Tiffany's face would split in two as she nodded. The brunette did a little dance, and all Meg could do was shake her head.

"It's been awhile, but man, he's got some kissing skills." Meg smiled, trying to tell herself she was just hamming it up for Tiffany's sake. But even the memory of it caused the nerves in her lips to go haywire.

Tiffany sat in a chair in front of Meg's desk. "So, you two are really dating. I'm sorry, I didn't believe you, but I guess it's true."

Meg tried to keep a neutral expression on her face, and it worked until Tiffany made faces. Scrunching her eyes closed, she said, "Who knows if it will last. I'm just worried he'll wake up one day and say, 'I've been dating you?'" Laying her head on her desk, she pretended to sob. But the words seemed to hit home more than she cared to admit.

"Please, you've been dating all of five days, and the man looks at you like you're the only woman on earth."

"He does not!" Meg tried to picture his expression, but she couldn't see anything different from normal. They hadn't known each other that long, and she was sure he had plenty of backstory when it came to relationships. Why else would someone need a fake girlfriend when he looked as good as he did?

Tiffany brought out her sassy side as she stood. "Girl, I was with you two for less than five minutes, and he didn't even act like I existed. Does he have a brother, by chance?"

Meg chuckled and stood, moving past Tiffany into the profile room. She took the seat behind the desk and pulled up the few matches she needed to finish by the end of the day.

"I think he does, but that's about all I know. I just found out he's going for his dad's partnership. And he has a stepmother."

"Well, Love Doctor, get to work and find out. This girl could use some eye candy for a good date."

Meg laughed until her stomach hurt. The bell from the front door rang, and she squeaked out, "Maybe you should get to work by seeing who that is. I need to get these people matched."

"This conversation isn't over," Tiffany said, as she walked out of the room. Meg heard a faint, male voice say, "Delivery for Meg Austen."

"Right this way." Tiffany's voice floated into the room. She walked in, eyes wide. Behind her looked like a large bouquet of flowers with a pair of legs.

The man behind the vase of white daisies moved it to the side and asked, "Where can I put these, Miss?"

As if frozen, Meg finally registered his words and pointed to the corner of the desk, filing several papers into her drawer to make room. He set the bottom of the vase on the desk and slowly pushed until the entire thing was a few inches from the edge. Standing, he pulled out a small electronic pad.

"If you'll just sign in the box and push accept, I'll be on my way." With a quick scribble, Meg nodded to him, and he left.

"Who's it from?" Tiffany practically hopped next to her.

Waving her off, Meg pulled the card out of the envelope and read, "So, you don't accuse me of never sending you flowers. Thanks again for your help last night. FB P."

Those darn flutters were back and in full force. And her heart. It beat wildly, as if it might work itself right out of her chest. She thought about the last time she received flowers and as she worked through boyfriends and special events like graduations, she realized no one had ever sent her flowers. Let alone her favorite kind.

"How does he know to send me daisies?" Meg narrowed her eyes in Tiffany's direction.

Raising a hand as if to block Meg's laser beams, Tiffany said, "Don't look at me. You were there when I met him." She paused a moment, probably to read the words on the card. "What does 'FB' stand for?"

Meg sucked in a long breath, panic taking over any coherent thoughts she might have had. "It, uh, is an inside joke. It really won't be funny to you because it was one of those, 'you-had-to-be-there' moments." She was the worst liar.

Tiffany frowned, her eyebrow raised as if Meg was insane. Shaking her head, Meg turned back to the flowers, the mystery of his choice still eating at her.

"Could be a lucky guess." She paused for a minute, trying to think like Parker.

"Or maybe he just called up the florist and asked what the best option for a new girlfriend would be." Tiffany folded her arms against her chest, raising an eyebrow as if she'd won. "It's on our sign. Maybe that was the tip. But isn't that the flower you send to someone who's sick?"

Meg laughed, thinking of the moment in *You've Got Mail* when the love interest brings the main character daisies. "Actually, it can symbolize new beginnings. It's one of the reasons I put it in the logo."

"I've never seen you get flowers before. I'd say you struck gold in more ways than one with the divorce lawyer. Has he ever been a model?"

"I'm not sure, but I'm not asking him that, especially if I have to bug him about his little brother for you. Keep your thoughts focused on him."

They both froze when they heard the bell ring again. A male voice called, "Hello?" Tiffany scrambled to her feet and out the office door. After a minute or two, Tiffany stood at the door. "New client," she mouthed.

Meg stood, picking up the vase of flowers and almost

dropped them when it was heavier than she expected. Two dozen daisies, and she felt like they weighed more than a twenty-five pound bag of flour.

She made it to the table to the right of her desk, where several of the brochures and cards sat, placing the flowers in the middle. When she let go, her left pointer finger cramped. She turned to focus on the man at the doorway. He was short and stout, with a touch of gray in his sideburns.

Tiffany looked as though she were trying to keep a neutral expression, but she kept looking over at the flowers. "Meg, this is Spencer Fry. He'd like to hear more about our program."

Trying to compose herself, Meg tucked some loose hair behind her ears and patted the messy bun, hoping it didn't look like she hadn't tried to get ready. New clients always made her a little self-conscious, especially the ones who'd been referred to her by friends.

"Of course. Welcome." She nodded to her assistant, more of a dismissal than anything. "Thank you, Tiffany."

Meg shook the man's hand over her desk and gestured for him to sit down with the other. "How can I help you today, Mr. Fry?"

"That's quite a lovely bouquet. Someone special in your life?" He pointed to the daisies over her shoulder.

Meg looked at the cheery flowers and sighed. "No. I mean yes!" The last word came out in a screech. "I'm sorry. It's a newer relationship from the past couple of months. I'm still getting used to it."

"That must be why you don't have pictures of him anywhere." The man pointed to a few of the walls and gestured to her desk, Meg's eyes following each movement. Her mind spun with all the excuses she could give but only one of them made it out.

"We moved into this building just a few weeks ago, and

I'm still trying to get everything unpacked, but that is something to put on my to-do list for sure." She picked up a pen and wrote on a Post-It note, "Pictures of the boyfriend."

Her eyes connected with the fake couple in the silver frame, and she grimaced. The price was still visible in the bottom corner. She turned it slightly in the hopes he wouldn't see the tag.

After going through the whole spiel, she ushered Mr. Fry into the testing room. When Meg explained they'd need references of people to contact, he was reluctant at first. She had given the "references-help-us-fill-out-your-profile" speech so many times, she could have done it in her sleep. He finally relented, and Meg held a paper with three references. When he left, he looked pleased and eager to find out who he'd be matched with.

The one thing that surprised her was his interest in younger women. He'd made it clear more than a few times that he wanted to be matched with women in their early twenties. That was a new one, but she was up for the challenge.

The office was quiet with Tiffany out to lunch, and the flowers drew her attention. The mixed emotions she felt as she looked at them made her want to drink in the smell and then throw them against the wall.

She shouldn't be so excited about flowers from a guy who she'd been dating less than a week. Check that. Fake dating. But she should probably tell him thank you.

Her cell phone vibrated against the desk, and Meg picked it up. Seeing Parker's name, she smiled. Maybe his ears were burning from her thoughts of him.

"I was just going to call you. These flowers are amazing. You didn't have to send them."

She could hear Parker's now familiar chuckle on the other line. "I hoped you would like them. Even fake boyfriends need to do little things, right?" She laughed at how he whispered 'fake.' He must be at the office.

"How did you know daisies are my favorite?"

"They are? Lucky guess. You don't seem like the red rose type." She wanted to ask him what gave him that impression but remembered her time with Spencer Fry.

"I need your help with something. I just had a client in here who mentioned I had no pictures of my boyfriend up, and I thought we should plan a time to take some around the city? Does that sound lame?"

"No, I think it's a great idea. Nothing like having photo evidence we've been dating." His voice on the last word made Meg swoon. It sounded like he choked it out.

"Fake dating, of course. I don't even know if I'd know what real dating is like anymore." She made a face and pounded her forehead with her palm. He'd just sent her flowers. Wasn't that a sign? "What day works for you?"

There was a pause on the other line, and she waited, worried that all the playful banter would only lead to a rejection.

"How about Saturday? I'm a sub for a rowing group in the morning, but I could do something around ten. Does that work?"

"I can't believe you get up that early to work out on a Saturday. Is that why your arms are so strong? Are you even human?" She paced the small space in her office now and turned to bang her head against the wall. Why was she so bad at this?

A deep guttural laugh hit her ears, and Meg couldn't stop herself from joining in.

"A girl who values her sleep. I can understand that. Do you want me to pick you up?"

Meg thought about it for a second and as much as it would be nice to ride in his car again and avoid the strange smells of public transportation, it would be a pain for him to come all the way out of the city for them to go right back in.

"Nah, I can meet you downtown somewhere. What do you say we be tourists for the day?"

"I haven't done that in so long. I probably don't remember any of the history from our fair city." The way he said the words with a dramatic flair caused her grin to grow even wider.

"You're telling me. I'll text you when I'm on my way in, and we'll meet up somewhere."

After hanging up the phone, she stared at the flowers in front of her. Would she ever find someone who would do little things like this to show he cared? And be her boyfriend for real?

CHAPTER 17

The early April morning had been crisp and clear. Parker's time rowing on the Charles River was always one of the refreshing and renewing parts of his week. He checked his phone a few more times as he sat in the club-house, his muscles enjoying the reprieve in motion.

A text sounded, and Parker saw Meg's name.

I'm on the train. Meet me at Park Street?

Sounds good. I'll meet you in the Common.

He threw the rest of his clothes in his duffle bag and walked out to his car. To find a parking spot, he'd have to leave now and hope he made it before she did.

Someone pulled out two streets down just as he turned the corner. Taking one last look in the rearview mirror and smoothing out his wet hair, he fixed the collar on his polo shirt. There were only a few people out and about as he walked to the large city park known as Boston Common.

He sat on a park bench, trying to think of things they could do. The thought of it made him a little nervous. He hadn't had to plan a date in years.

"This isn't a date. This isn't a date. This is my due diligence to become a partner." He turned his head and saw Meg only a few steps away. He hoped she hadn't heard him. He'd learned to wait for her bright smiles and even though she was still beautiful when they talked about their past, he still preferred to make her happy.

"Good morning. How was your rowing at the crack of dawn?" She slid onto the bench next to him. Dressed in jeans that hugged her curves and a flowy, flowered top, her hair hung down in a loose wave. It was such a change to her ponytail or updo that he almost did a double take. She looked amazing, pulling at bits of a bagel and stuffing them in her mouth. Wow, she was attractive.

Cool your jets, Parker. You're just friends. For now.

The last two words threw him for a loop. He'd never even contemplated dating a girl longer than one date and yet he'd made it through a dinner with people he interacted with all the time, and she'd made it fun. He mentally calculated how much time they had left until the end of the month and wondered how he could extend that time for a week or two, maybe even indefinitely.

"It was good. You look nice this morning." He smiled at her, and she gave him a sheepish look.

She bit the side of her bottom lip, something he noticed she did often, usually after he complimented her. "Thanks. I thought about wearing sweats and a t-shirt."

"What stopped you? I could've gone for comfy."

"You? This is the most casual I've ever seen you, and you look like you could model your current outfit. By the way, Tiffany wanted me to ask you if you've ever been a model. My question is: do you even own a t-shirt?"

Parker cracked a smile. "Touché. And yes, I own several t-shirts, but suits and slacks are work attire. I have to wear a suit so often, a polo and jeans feels relaxed. But now I want to wear sweats." He paused, trying to remember all her questions. He smiled and said, "No, modeling… just, no."

She smiled, reaching up to fix the collar he thought he'd fixed. Her nearness brought a mixture of spring flowers and honey to his nose.

"Believe it or not, I know how to relax. That's what my Sundays are for." He stood up, holding out his hand for her. "What do you want to do today?"

"Let's follow the Freedom Trail. I haven't done it in years, and I figured there are several changes in scenery to help us mix up our pictures." She made a face, and Parker laughed.

The sound of her laugh sent a shiver down his back. He felt that string from the other day get just a hair thicker as he looked at her lips, making the pull toward her increase by ten times. Instead of acting on it, he took a step backwards, reminding himself she wasn't interested in anything more than their current arrangement.

He nodded and realized she was staring at him. "Sounds great. Oh, I might have told Ben we're dating. He sent me a text this morning to see if we want to meet them for dinner. Did you have any other plans?"

She shook her head and bobbed up and down. "Are you kidding? I haven't seen Lily since her wedding day. I'm in!" Her fist pumped high in the air, and then she moved it down, as if pointing in the direction they should go. Parker chuckled, taking her shoulders and turning her body around, pointing east.

"The start of the trail is that way," he whispered as he breathed in more of her honey scent. He let go of her shoulders and led the way to the beginning of the red bricks, laid throughout the city to signify the trail.

She caught up to him, trying to hide her smile. "Of course, I knew that. I was just testing you." They walked a few paces in silence when she stopped short. "Wait, we're eating dinner with Lily and Ben, as a real couple but a fake couple. Did that make sense?"

"Not really. We'll be fine though, right?"

Meg grimaced and dropped her head back, more dramatic than he'd ever seen her. "Lily is like a human lie detector. The only reason I got away with lying about my bridesmaid dress being perfect, was because it was her wedding day. When she's focused, I'm dead."

"You didn't like your dress, huh? I agree. The one you wore to dinner at Bart's was fantastic." Wrapping his arm around her shoulders, he took a step forward, pulling her along with him. "Let's have some fun today, and we'll worry about our friends when we see them, all right?" She rolled her lips in and gave him a side-eye glance.

"Okay, sounds like a plan."

* * *

HE COULDN'T REMEMBER a day when he'd laughed more as their journey along the trail flew by. Granted, his calves seized up once near the end, and he couldn't feel his feet anymore, but it was all worth it. To see the excitement in Meg's eyes at the Old North Church, or the U.S.S. Constitution made the wall he'd built around his heart weaken a little more.

She was so different from Courtney, taking things in stride rather than complaining throughout the entire process. He'd stopped planning outdoor excursions that didn't involve some sort of shopping near the end of his relationship with Courtney because it wasn't worth the trouble of dragging her along with him. He should have seen that as a sign long before the thoughts of proposing came to him.

Occasionally, Meg would tell him to lean in, and she would snap a photo. Sometimes he'd make a face, and she'd make one too, sending them into fits of laughter. It was something Courtney had never done. Just one more check in the Meg column, if he was keeping score. Which he wasn't.

As they made it back to Park Street, he said, "My car's over here. My legs are dead."

Meg moved back and forth like a boxer, not as graceful, but it made him smile. "Are you a little tired, Parker?"

"Well, while you were getting more beauty sleep, I was working out my guns." He flexed his right bicep and couldn't help but laugh as her jaw dropped open. She snapped it shut within a few seconds, trying to mask the surprised expression.

"Okay. Point taken. Maybe I should do a little working out of my own. I thought my legs were going to fall off once we got to the U.S.S. Constitution."

Only lifting one side of his mouth, Parker tried to say with a straight face, "Why didn't you say something? I could've carried you the rest of the way."

She punched him in the shoulder and then again in the chest. They'd made it to the car, and she turned, rolling her eyes at him. She opened the door of his car for herself, sliding in before he had the chance to make it around.

Once he got into the driver seat, Meg said, "That was a lot of fun."

Parker pulled out of his parking spot and headed through some side streets. He nodded. "Yes, it was. I haven't taken time to enjoy the city since before law school."

"Did you love her?"

"Law school?" It was a small joke, but the question turned his insides as if someone had punched him in the gut. He'd been comparing Meg to Courtney all afternoon but talking about his ex made him uncomfortable.

She smiled and shook her head. "The girl you proposed to."

"Well, I did propose. That usually translates into, 'I thought about our future together.'"

"Did it take you a long time to get over her?" Her serious expression made him wonder what had spurred this conversation.

Blowing out a deep breath, he tried to concentrate on the road. "I remember it was almost a year before my feelings for her disappeared."

"What if she showed up tomorrow? Do you think you'd get back together with her?"

Parker frowned. "This is a little intense for a fake date, don't you think?"

Meg looked down at her hands. "I'm sorry. Drawbacks of my job. I'm always trying to dig deeper into my client's life that I sometimes forget I've gone too far." She paused, lifting her gaze to him. "I wonder if my life would have been different if my father hadn't died. Would my mom still have become the person she is now?"

They let the moment hang between them before he said, "No." She turned to look at him, her eyes welling up with tears. Realizing she'd taken his answer to be for her last question, he rushed on. "I'm a different person now. I'd like to think I wouldn't get back together with her."

He reached over and touched her hand, rubbing his thumb back and forth over the back of it as he drove. The action reminded him of her doing it at Bart's to help calm him down. It seemed to have the same effect on her. Sneaking a glance, he found her with a slight smile on her face. Something felt more than right about this. But how could he tell her that without scaring her away?

When Parker pulled in front of Ralph's Burgers, Meg mentally kicked herself. What was her deal, and why had she asked him all those personal questions? She was his *fake* girlfriend.

Just because they'd had an amazing day together, didn't mean he'd be ripped away from her like every other thing she'd loved. Or liked. Because she liked him as a good friend. Sort of. He'd be leaving as soon as the terms of their contract were filled, and she just needed to accept that fact, even though her heart had somehow disconnected communications from her brain.

He came around the car. "Are you all right?"

"Of course." She tried to make her voice sound happy but noticed the quaver. "I studied psychology in college. Sometimes I ask too many questions and forget how personal they are until they've already slipped out of my mouth. Should we eat?"

"Yes, please. You starved us today." Meg looked back at him as she walked through the door to find a mischievous grin on his face. She went on tiptoe, trying to find Lily and

Ben. There were a lot of people in the diner, and she couldn't see much.

Turning to Parker, she said, "Okay, tall one. The mission is to find our friends."

He shook his head as he looked out over the booths. "I see Lily in the back corner." Meg practically ran in the direction he pointed and swallowed Lily up in a bear hug.

"How was the honeymoon? When did you get back?" Meg breathed in, feeling a little more at balance with her best friend there.

"It was amazing. We did one of those scuba diving excursions and saw so many fish. Luckily, no sharks. But it was good inspiration for a new piece I've been trying to figure out." Lily broke away and saw Parker standing behind Meg. She leaned in a little closer and whispered, "We need to talk about this new relationship."

When she stepped back, Meg forced a smile as she slid into the booth first. Talking to Lily about her relationship with Parker was the last thing she wanted to do, especially if she was to keep it a secret.

Ben came around the corner and slid in beside Lily. Parker stuck out his hand, and the two of them tried to arm wrestle.

"Is this your method of greeting each other?" Meg asked, giggling nervously. Again with the bulging muscles. It was like a show Meg couldn't tear her eyes from. And since Parker was wearing a polo, she could see every bit.

It was Lily who finally said, "Okay, boys, we don't want to give the whole restaurant a show. Besides, I'm famished."

As if on cue, Meg's stomach rumbled in response, and she laughed. "Sounds like my stomach could use some sustenance as well."

Parker rolled his eyes. "Should we be drinking tea and eating biscuits now?" He smirked, and Meg slapped his bicep with the back of her hand. Bad idea. Was this guy made of steel or something?

"Oh, Meg. I've missed you." She turned her head and said, "Parker, you haven't seen anything yet. We need to have a Jane Austen marathon." Her eyes lit up, and Meg laughed when Ben laid his head down on the table, more dramatic than usual.

"How about the two of you do the marathon? I need to watch an action movie before Lily dresses me like some of the male characters in those chick flicks."

"I can't say I've seen any of the movies," Parker said. Lily stared at him like he'd just emerged from a spaceship.

Looking between Meg and Parker, her gaze mischievous, Lily said, "We'll fix that tonight. Come over, and we can educate you on the ways of wooing women."

Meg's eyes glanced around the restaurant. No holes to duck into. She could use an invisibility cloak right about now.

"So, when did you two start dating?" Lily lowered her eyes, trying to look serious. Meg kicked her under the table.

Parker saved the day by leaning forward and whispering, "We aren't telling many people, but since you two are the reason we met, we've decided to move to Oregon."

A chorus of "What?" from the table caused Parker to laugh, throwing his hands up. "I'm just kidding."

"We met at your wedding, actually. He asked me to dance, and we got to talking and—"

"And I asked her out for the next day. It's been a great week." He looked at her when he said it, his expression soft. Meg gulped, wondering if those sky-blue eyes were holding her in a trance. It would be a good life if that were all she had to do every day.

"How's matchmaking, Meg?" Ben asked as he studied the menu.

Breaking her stare, Meg stretched her hands forward. "I'm in the process of getting investors, I hope."

Lily leaned forward, her chin on her hand. "I hadn't heard you were trying to get investors, Meg. You saved for forever. Is business down?"

Not wanting to talk about this in front of the two guys, Meg squirmed in her seat, pretending to study the menu. "No, business is steadily increasing. But now with office rent, the renovations we did to the office, and the program Jorge designed for me, we're a little short on money to develop the app."

Ben, always the conservative type, said, "Why don't you wait a few more months to get started on it?"

"Because it takes months to develop, and then there is beta testing and other work that goes into it, I'm sure. The sooner it's launched, that's just one more avenue Love, Austen will reach people. On a global scale."

"It can't be much to develop an app though, right?" Lily asked.

Meg nodded. This wasn't a conversation she wanted to have with two people who'd never had to worry about money on the scale she had. She opened her mouth to respond but before she could say anything, Parker piped up.

"It depends on how intricate you want to make it. Those quote-of-the-day type apps are simple and don't require a lot of interfacing or backend work, meaning it's cheaper. For an app to benefit a matchmaking company, with the options that would have to be created, you're talking upwards of six figures."

Both Lily and Ben's mouths dropped open. Meg just pointed to Parker as if that were enough to confirm all he'd said. She could picture the small blue paper in her desk drawer, the quote well over a million for all the little options and backend work.

"It's a big investment, but with everyone using smart-phones and tablets these days, it can connect people from around the world, not just the ones here in Boston."

Lily used her hands as she spoke. "But Meg, I've watched you work. How would you be able to match so many people by yourself?"

"A tighter algorithm and an updated program that Jorge is working on. Tiffany and I have been testing other methods, and those have proven successful. It would eliminate shadowing the client for a whole day and frees us up a lot of time for other things."

Meg took a sip of water, trying to moisten the desert in her mouth. She hated talking business with these two. Both Lily and Ben were the kindest people she knew, but they'd been given a lot and came from well-off families. She'd been surprised Parker knew so much about the app-building process though.

"Jorge has several people who could help with creating the app, but funds start things. I have to do it, though. My business doesn't depend on it yet but if I ever want a family, I can't be sitting in an office for sixteen hours a day trying to match up people."

Lily gasped. "Did you actually say you wanted a family?" The shock in Lily's voice made Meg shiver. She could feel Parker's eyes on her, but she stared at her glass, drawing circles in the residue water on the table.

Meg was so relieved when the waitress finally showed up to their table. Lily and Ben split the giant breakfast, and Parker ordered a bacon cheeseburger and fries. Meg looked at him as she tried to make her final decision.

"I'll have what he's having." Maybe a little fat would ease the knots in her stomach from the interrogation.

CHAPTER 19

"How was that?" he asked, trying to keep his voice soft, even though Lily and Ben weren't within earshot anymore. They were walking back to the car, and Meg breathed a sigh of relief.

"After the interrogation ended, it was great." She turned her head to look at the nearly black sky. "I rarely talk business in front of them. They don't get the whole 'owning-your-own-business' thing." She looked down and walked next to him, her hands stuffed into her pockets. "Thanks for helping me with the app stuff. That's something they'll always question."

"I only know about that from a friend who built that popular fitness app. What's it called?"

"Fitness Overhaul?"

Parker snapped his fingers. "That's it. I couldn't believe it cost that much to create, but he's made triple what he invested on it."

"Then there's hope for me yet." She flashed him a smile before she bumped into him with her elbow. If her hand weren't in her pocket, he'd probably reach out to hold it. It was getting to the point where he felt lost when she wasn't touching him.

"Are you sure you want to head to their place?" He hoped his voice carried the dread he felt.

She sat up and looked over at him. "Yeah, it will be fun. If we get tired, we'll sneak out. Chances are high they'll both fall asleep within the first half of the movie."

Parker raised his eyebrows. "Why bother then?"

Meg moved her mouth to the side, looking thoughtful. "That's a good question. It's been a long time since I've done anything but work and hang out with them."

The drive to Ben and Lily's didn't take long and soon enough, he was snuggled next to Meg on the couch.

"Are we really watching this? How did I end up here, preparing to watch a girl show?" Parker winked at Meg. She gave him a close-mouthed smile, leaning her head on his shoulder. Ben threw them a blanket as he sat next to Lily, who'd sprawled out on the bigger couch.

"Well, if you want a future with that girl next to you, it's good to educate yourself on her favorite things in life. She watched these movies so many times our senior year, I was sure she could have been a one-woman play," Lily said, giggling.

Meg laughed and shook her head. "It was in the name of research." She dramatized the last few words, causing everyone to crack up. "To be honest, I had to take a long break from them after that. I think I've only seen *Pride and Prejudice* once in the last four years."

The microwave beeped, and Lily hopped up and ran to the kitchen. Ben worked to get the movie started and paused it to wait for her return. Holding four bowls, she handed one to each person and gave the bag of microwave popcorn to Parker. "Take some and pass it down."

He poured some into his bowl and dumped some into

Meg's until popcorn spilled out the sides. "You're supposed to say 'when.'"

She gave him a side smirk and took a handful, dumping it into Lily's bowl. The newlyweds were busy splitting up the rest of the popcorn when Parker turned to Meg.

"Okay, big question. Microwave or theater popcorn?"

"I'd have to say microwave." She made a face with her teeth clenched, waiting for his response.

"Really? That surprises me."

"Why? I haven't been to the movies often in the past few years. Maybe I just don't remember what it tastes like." She raised an eyebrow as she popped a few kernels in her mouth.

Parker grinned. "I never said I liked theater popcorn better. I'm a microwave man myself."

Meg poked him in the side with a finger, and Parker doubled over, his laugh low enough she must not have heard him at first. "What? Are you all right?"

"Just a bit ticklish there," he said. Her face beamed and this time, she used both hands, going for his stomach. Parker jerked back and moved, trying to get her to stop, but she ducked out of the way and kept poking his side. She pulled back, pulling hair away from her eyes, and smiled at him. They were both out of breath, but their eyes locked, and her smile softened. He leaned in just a little, ready to feel the soft touch of her lips when Lily shushed them from the next seat over.

"Okay, lovebirds. I thought newlyweds were supposed to be bad. Shut up and love this movie. I mean you, Parker." She made a motion from her eyes to his, and he pretended to zip his lips together.

Meg poked him one last time before leaning into him, eating her popcorn. He could get used to this.

It wasn't long before he could hear the soft snores as her head cuddled in the crook of his neck. Moving his arm out from the blanket, he put it around her head, running his fingers through her hair. It was so soft and silky. With every stroke, a whiff of her orange shampoo hit him, and he wished for this night to never end.

Cuddling a beautiful, spunky girl with a smile that could light the rest of his life, he felt his attraction to her deepen. They'd only known each other a week, so it couldn't possibly be love.

A strong like, then.

He had to tell her how he felt. But could it wait until after their agreement was over? He pushed it from his mind, determined to enjoy this moment.

CHAPTER 20

As the girls hugged goodbye, Parker stood next to Ben on the sidewalk. It was near midnight, and he'd been the only one to stay awake and watch the entire show.

Now that everyone was awake, he figured he'd ask a question that had been bugging him since dinner. Glancing over to make sure Meg wasn't listening, he leaned in closer to Ben.

"Why was Lily so shocked at dinner about Meg wanting to have a family?"

Ben side-glanced to his wife and tilted his head to Parker. "Has she told you a lot about her childhood?"

"Bits and pieces, but not much."

Letting out a slow breath, Ben looked over at the girls again when he spoke. "Her mom grieved her father for about a month as far as I gather. Then she went out all the time, dating a lot of random men. She married and divorced a few. I think Lily said she even tried to date one of Meg's boyfriends in high school."

Studying Meg as she laughed at something Lily said, Parker tried to picture her as a young girl, trying to figure out her role in the world. He saw pure enjoyment on her face now, but how long had it taken to get there? "That still doesn't explain why she wouldn't want a family."

"She worries that she'll lose them too. A couple of years after her father died, the bank took the house. They lived with her mom's parents for several years until they both died. I think the grandma died freshman year of college, and Lily said Meg didn't take it well. I think a part of her feels like anything and anyone she loves will be taken away." Ben took a breath and smiled. "You two are quite the pair, aren't you? She worries that she'll lose who she loves, and you think all women leave."

The words stabbed Parker in the stomach, the realization all too clear now. He'd never thought of it as simply as Ben had just described, but it was more accurate than he cared to admit. He must have been lost in his thoughts because Ben's next statement brought him back to the present.

"She seems to really like you, though. Maybe against her better judgment." Ben grinned and slapped Parker on the back. Even though his friend was two inches shorter, he was strong, and Parker held back a wince.

"What do you mean?"

Ben shrugged. "The day Meg found out Steve was cheating on her, she resolved to avoid men."

"For how long?"

"There was no set time limit. But for how stubborn she's been ever since, it's still a bit of a shock you two hit it off so well. If Lily had known, she would've forced me to play matchmaker for the two of you."

Biting the inside of his cheek, Parker stared at Meg once again. "Her talking about having a family is a good sign, right?"

"I would think it's good. But, then again, ask her yourself. Don't make the same mistake you did with Courtney."

Parker felt his defenses rise, cool air raising the hairs on his neck. Keeping his voice low, he demanded, "What mistake?"

"You two never talked about the future. And there was no way she wanted to have kids. I know you've done your own blocking of women, but you've always been good with kids. It's something to discuss early on, so you don't waste your time with different opinions."

All the air went out of him as his mind tried to recall any sign that what Ben said was true. With his friend's track record on hitting things on the nose, Parker knew it was true. A bitter taste rose in his throat.

"I'm ready for bed, Benny." Lily slipped her arms around his waist and laid her head on his shoulder. "It's late, and these two have been gallivanting around the city all day. They probably don't want to hear any more about our amazing honeymoon." She leaned up, and he kissed her on the lips.

Meg took Parker's hand, and he turned to see her smile at their friends. This was the best chance he'd gotten since he'd kissed her in front of Tiffany, and he wouldn't miss it. Turning towards her, he moved to cup her face in his hands, kissing her lips with a feather-like touch. She leaned into him, and he pulled her closer, the kiss intensifying. His mind clouded over, and it wasn't until he heard a grunt from the others that he pulled back.

Meg's eyes were still closed and as she opened them, she looked either ready to fall asleep or a little drunk from the kiss. He hoped it was the latter. His chest burst into flames, and he wondered how long it had been since he'd felt like this. Never. Never had a kiss turned his legs to jelly.

Lily's mouth dropped wide open, and Ben chuckled. She gave Meg one last hug, and Parker overheard her whisper, "Lunch tomorrow. You've got some explaining to do, missy."

Turning his head so she wouldn't think he'd overheard, they all said goodbye as Meg and Parker got in his car.

Meg's fingers touched her lips as she stared at the dashboard.

"Sorry, I got a little carried away."

As if startling back to reality, she said, "Huh? Oh, I think it was a convincing, um, you know." Her words came out breathy, and Parker felt his ego raise its head at least an inch.

"Oh, before I forget, here is the card of a caterer I highly recommend. You still need one, right?"

Meg looked at the card as if it might blow away if she touched it. "You didn't have to find someone. How did you remember?"

"I wasn't sure if you'd found one, and she's a friend from law school."

"And she caters?" Meg raised an eyebrow.

"She left the program after the first year. Her words were that she could cook better than interrogate. I bumped into her a few days ago and asked if she'd be up to the job."

He paused a second and smirked, the impatience registering high on her face. "And?" she asked.

"And she can do it. Just give her a call, and you can figure out details."

She lunged toward Parker, and her lips found his for a quick second, before she sat back in her seat, all smiles. Everything happened so fast, he wondered if he'd imagined it. If she could get so excited about something so small, he wouldn't mind helping her the rest of her life. Or, the rest of the month. Because that was the goal, right?

He began to think a fake relationship might not have been the best idea. The month would end soon, and he wasn't sure if he'd make it out with his whole heart.

CHAPTER 21

Two days later, as Meg sat in the back room of her office, finding matches for some newer Captain Wentworth clients, she still couldn't get that kiss out of her mind. She was in trouble and boy, was it bad.

How could she let herself have feelings for Parker? It wasn't hard to see why women flocked to him with his gorgeous eyes and chiseled jaw. But there was a vulnerability there, and it seemed like he needed her as much as she needed him, and not just for the fake relationship.

But then again, was she reading too much into it? Had the kiss just been for a reaction from Lily and Ben?

She'd felt like they were flying, the sensation of his lips on hers made her toes curl. When he pulled her closer to him, those strong arms made her feel safe. Protected. But would they always be there for her?

Her cell phone rang with a number she didn't recognize. On a normal day, she would have let it go to voicemail, but she was so lost in thought, she swiped to connect the call.

"Hello, this is Meg."

A nasally voice came through the line in a thick Boston accent. "Is this Meg Austen?"

"Yes. May I ask who's calling?"

"I'm a producer at the show, *Everything Your Heart Desires*, where we feature the newest trends in fashion, restaurants, as well as up-and-coming businesses, like yours. I received a tip that Love, Austen would make a great piece for our show. Would you be willing to come on and talk about it?"

Meg pulled the phone away from her ear and stared at it, trying to decide if she was asleep or not. "Yes, I can do that. What day?"

"We need you at the station at eleven Thursday morning."

Trying not to seem too eager, she paused, opening her calendar even though she knew she was available. "Yes, that should work. You'll send me the details?"

"Yes, ma'am." The woman hung up the phone, and Meg let out a shriek.

Tiffany ran into the room, concern in her eyes. "Everything okay in here?"

Meg held out her phone, as if it would tell her assistant all that had just transpired. "I got a call from that daytime talk show in Boston, *Everything Your Heart Desires*. They want me to come on the show Thursday."

Tiffany jumped up and down, and Meg joined in. "This is so exciting! I can't believe you'll be on TV. Nothing better than free advertising." She sat on the chair next to Meg. "Are you going to tell Parker?"

The question threw her off guard. She was so used to sharing all her good news with Lily. Had Parker taken her place?

"Maybe if it comes up in conversation. I haven't talked to him since Saturday, so we'll see." Now realizing that two days had gone by, she wondered why he hadn't at least texted her.

Was she a bad kisser? But the way he'd looked at her, there was no way he wasn't feeling sparks too, right?

Parker's face came up on her phone. Did he have a radar that detected every time she talked about him?

"Hey, there."

"Hey, yourself. I don't have a ton of time to talk, and I feel bad about this, but what are you doing tonight?"

Meg tried to keep from smiling. "What do you feel bad about? I mean, we are dating, of course."

"I keep asking you to come to my work things and I feel like I haven't held up my end of the bargain for you. Don't you need me to come to anything?"

She'd been expecting to hear from the investors, but there had been no missed calls or any notice they would meet her soon. Worry hit her like an elephant with a bowling ball.

Wow, I didn't think it was possible for me to get worse with those. No more comparisons.

"I really haven't heard much. But I'll keep you posted." She tucked a piece of hair behind her ear. "Now, what's going on tonight?"

"We're volunteering to cook dinner for the children's hospital. Do you want to come?"

She hesitated. Lily and Ben visited and read to the children there often. But it was harder for Meg, and the worry of connecting and then losing the kids to cancer or their other sicknesses made it harder for her to go. But if this would help as part of the fake girlfriend job description, she would hold up her end of the bargain.

"Sure. What time?"

"I'll pick you up at five."

Hanging up the phone, Meg wondered what she'd just agreed to and if her heart could handle it.

* * *

As she got into Parker's car, Meg saw something out of the corner of her eye on the floor just behind Parker's seat. A copy of *Emma*.

"What's this for?" She held it up where Parker could see as he buckled his seatbelt.

With an awkward grin, he said, "I was a little curious after the movie the other night. So, I started reading it."

Meg couldn't help but smile wide. "And? What do you think?"

He ran a hand through his hair, causing a little section to stick straight up. For some reason, she loved watching him do that, knowing it was a way for him to gather his thoughts before he answered.

"It's good so far. Some parts are a little boring with all the descriptions, but I'm at the part where Mr. Elton brings back his new bride."

A giggle escaped her lips, and Meg clapped her hand against her mouth. "Oh man! She's a character, isn't she?"

With a nod, he said, "That she is. I wondered how Emma couldn't see Elton's advances."

"She's so focused on matching him up with Miss Smith, she just interpreted his advances to his interest in the younger girl."

"Did he even have a chance with her? Say he likes her and decides he wants to take the relationship to the next level, whatever that next level was in those times—"

"Courting. The next level was courting."

"Okay, what if he made his sentiments known—oh wow! I'm starting to talk like the characters." He shook his head and all Meg could do was laugh, but the sound came out more like a cackle.

After they settled down a bit, he sobered, trying to decide

how to express his thoughts. "What if he told her how he'd felt before Miss Smith came into the picture?" Parker narrowed his eyes at her as if it were a challenge.

Tapping her finger against her lips, Meg had never thought of that before. "It's a good question. Emma says she'll probably never marry, but I guess it was just a matter of realizing who she really cared for in the end."

"So, you're saying the guy has to do everything he can to make her see he likes her and then just hope for the best?"

Twirling a piece of hair around her finger, Meg couldn't think of a good answer to that. "Well, it's not really fair when it's one-sided, but I don't know. I'm sure that was all that could be done in Jane's time. But now, I think it's important for both to admit to their feelings."

"Do you always admit yours?"

The question made her stop and turn to look at him. "No, I guess not. I don't want to say I've gone through a lot, because when I think about the kids and families we're about to see, my pain is a small drop in the bucket. But I've gone through a lot that makes me wary to divulge everything."

Silence took over for a moment as they mulled over the conversation. She couldn't read his expression, and it niggled at her. Remembering something, she turned to him.

"I got some prints back from our citywide excursion. I was going to hang them today, but I ran out of time."

"Did you make any extra for me?" He flashed her a smile that sent her heart a pitter-patter.

"Maybe. I'll make sure to bring you some. Are you sure you want them? We look kind of crazy." With a close-lipped grin, she waited for his answer.

"Those are the best kind. Besides, it might be a good idea for me to put some on my desk, you know, just in case anyone asks about you."

She gave him a fake frown. "Of course, they're going to ask about me. They'll say, 'Who's the amazing girl who puts up with Parker's teasing?'" Her laugh echoed against the walls of the car until Parker's joined in.

"Did you call Lexi?"

Meg narrowed her eyes at him. "Lexi who?"

"The caterer. Did you get it all worked out?"

Feeling a surge of excitement, she sat up and turned in her seat as much as the belt would allow her. "I did. She sounds like a total find. I told her what I wanted for the main menu, mostly traditional stuff to keep with the theme. I let her take care of the desserts."

"Good choice. She's a fabulous baker. I'm hoping for some tres leches."

"Tres whaties?"

"Tres leches. Translated from Spanish, it means 'three milks.' It's a dessert from Mexico, and the cake is super moist."

"She told me she's from Peru." Meg's stomach seized up. Had she made a mistake not directing what to make?

Parker laughed and must have read her mind because he said, "She was born in Peru, but she'd lived here since she was younger. She makes desserts from several countries, and I tried a bunch of them when she first started cooking in law school. Those were some of the best study sessions I'd ever had. I had to work out a lot come Monday mornings."

Meg pushed the mental picture of him aside. After their tickling session, she was sure he'd been genetically modified.

"Okay, I'll keep it the way it is. But if things go bad, and my guests don't like them, I'm holding you responsible."

"Honey, you can hold me anytime." He winked at her, and she backhanded his shoulder, rolling her eyes. Secretly, she loved his witty banter. But seconds after, she always felt the caution of her heart beating out. *Be careful.*

Parker entered the parking garage of the hospital, finding a spot on the first level.

All the lightheartedness floated away. She knew why they were here, and she blew out a long breath. What had she done?

Pulling the key out of the ignition, Parker turned to her. "Can I ask you a question?"

"Sure."

"Are you okay being here? You seemed a little hesitant on the phone, and I don't want you to do something you don't want to. Do you not like kids?"

She felt her eyes fly open. "Oh, no, I love kids. I guess, well, I have a lot of baggage and occasionally, it trips me up. Hey, that analogy wasn't half-bad."

He chuckled, but it ended short. He didn't want to cause a tangent from her answer.

"Seeing sick kids reminds me of when my dad was sick. It's like a signal that because they're sick, or have cancer, or some other disease, that I'll lose them. So, instead of trying to comfort them, I stay away."

She saw his jaw working, and he didn't look totally convinced. "Do you want me to take you home?"

With a shake of the head, she said, "No, let's go in. I'm learning that change is sometimes good, even if it's uncomfortable at first."

She pulled on the door handle and walked over to him, slipping her hand into his. Just like clockwork, the electric pulse flew up her arm. "Might as well walk in connected."

He grinned, and she saw his shoulders relax. What had been bugging him? She could appreciate the tactful way he'd approached the kids subject. They may not be real-dating, but it was something she'd want to know if she were to see a future with someone.

She thought of the caterer and the book in his car. He was

a lot more than she'd expected him to be. Instead of the flat divorce lawyer she'd pegged him as, she saw the intelligent, thoughtful, and kind man he was. Not to mention hot. But she'd better keep that one to herself.

She might have to rethink the whole man-free diet.

CHAPTER 22

Thursday came bright and early. After a wonderful evening of cooking and serving the grateful families at the hospital, Meg had thanked Parker over and over for inviting her. The thrill of serving someone who wasn't paying her was something new, and she had to find a way to replicate the feeling. Plus, the look on Connor's face when she walked in was priceless. He hadn't brought Samantha, and he kept sending her nasty glances.

Since then, she and Parker had texted back and forth several times. Each time she heard the ding on her phone, she grabbed it like a lovesick puppy, excitement filling her with every flirty comment or funny joke.

As she pulled out a pair of black slacks and pulled them on, she realized she'd forgotten to tell him about the talk show. It didn't directly relate to their relationship, but it still impacted her business. They'd shared several other details, and she should probably tell him this. She made a mental note to call him while she was on the bus.

Throwing on a pastel-blue top, the sleeves flowy and flowers embroidered along the neckline, she ran the straightener over the few waves in her hair before pulling out the black heels she'd worn to Parker's work dinner the week before and put them in her bag. She'd wear her black flats until she arrived, so she didn't want to cry within the first hour of the day.

Just as she got on the bus, she recognized the manager of her office building's phone number. She mentally thought about the date, wondering why he would call her. It was only the second week of the month.

"Hi George. How are you?"

A loud noise came from behind him, and his voice sounded muffled. "Not good. Today isn't a good day."

"Is there something I can help you with?" She tried to make her voice as helpful as possible. George was older, a little grumpy, but she'd been on his good side since she'd volunteered to take on the repairs of the office building for a lower monthly lease, and she wanted to keep it that way.

A grunt sounded through the other line as he pulled something free. "Your first floor is covered in six inches of water."

"Wait, what?" Her heart sped up as she tried to slow her breathing, hoping this was all a big joke.

"A pipe burst in the building next door. I came in to check on that light switch you said was out, and there's water everywhere."

Sinking down into a seat between an older gentleman and a young teenage boy, Meg leaned forward on her knees and tried to keep from crying.

"I'm on the bus now," she said, looking at her watch. "I'll come by before my appointment." She reached up to push the yellow strip on the wall, alerting the driver to let her off at the next stop. Pausing, she asked, "George, is it bad?"

He made a grunting noise and said, "It sure is, sweetheart. I've called my insurance, but alert your renter's insurance company just to be safe. The neighbors are at fault, but you never know how that will turn out."

He clicked off the phone, and a knot twisted back and forth in her stomach, pressing up on her lungs, taking the breath with it. After a change of transportation and a quick call to the insurance company, she arrived at the office.

Her mind seemed to have unraveled as she walked in the door thirty minutes after George first called her. Her heart lifted as she noticed the water wasn't as high as it had been, a faint line on the wall showing her it had been at least three inches higher at one point.

George pulled a shop vacuum behind him as he worked to suck up the water in the lobby.

"How are things in the back room?" She looked in that direction, hoping the damage hadn't risen to ruin the monitors.

"I haven't been back there yet. Go look."

Meg ground her teeth together, rolling up her slacks to her knees, and trudged through the ankle-high water to the back room. Turning on the system, she was grateful to see that none of it had sustained damage with everything on the wall mounted waist high. She opened the supply closet, grateful she'd splurged for all the totes.

She walked back out to George. "I have a meeting I can't miss downtown, but I'll come here straight after. Do you have somewhere we can go while things get cleaned up?" She'd been doing this business without an office for so long, but the convenience of having a one-stop location made her worry about people missing her business.

"I'll ask around. We'll have the insurance adjusters look to assess damage. You might air it out and continue business, or they might tear out the walls to replace the sheetrock. I'm sorry about this, sweetheart." George gave her a look that reminded her of her grandfather.

As she walked out the door, her feet and socks soaked, she started a new text to Tiffany.

We'll need a backup base of operations for a couple more weeks. Will you look into that while I'm at the interview?

I'm on it. It was just one more reason Tiffany needed a raise.

Walking across the street to the T-stop, Meg sat heavily on the bench. She still had at least ten people to match up from last week and after today's interview, she hoped they'd have dozens more. Not to mention all the final preparations for the gala next week. Her stress level was at an all-time high, but she'd just have to function on little to no sleep.

"Just one more thing." she said, her head leaned back and eyes closed, waiting for the train to come.

Parker walked into the building of WCVB, the channel broadcasting the *Everything Your Heart Desires* show. Part of him couldn't understand why an afternoon talk show aimed at women wanted to interview him. The producer had been rather vague yesterday on the phone, but he lacked that critical puzzle piece to link everything together.

After the receptionist sent him through, a woman asked, "Name?" Her dark, curly hair piled on top of her head and a headset with a microphone covered her mouth.

"Parker Matthews."

The woman looked down at her clipboard and then behind him, a crease forming on her forehead. "Where's the girl?"

"Excuse me? What girl are you talking about?"

"Your girlfriend. It says right here your interview is with Meg Austen."

Parker held up a finger and said, "Let me see about that."

How had he not known she'd be here? They'd spent the evening together at the hospital, and it had been fantastic.

With all the texts sent back and forth in the days since, he was surprised she hadn't brought it up. Was she hiding this from him? Or did it just slip her mind?

Whoa. She's not hiding things from me. You didn't tell her either.

He felt all the familiar anger boiling up inside, and he took a few deep breaths, cooling it to lukewarm. Why did it matter anyway? It's not like they were a real couple.

And that's what cut him the most, that as much as he was feeling for this girl, he wasn't sure she would return the affection after this whole charade was over.

Walking a few steps away, he dialed Meg. The curtness of her voice surprised him.

"Sorry, this isn't the best time to talk. The train got stuck on the track, and now I'm late for an interview."

"With *Everything Your Heart Desires*?" he asked, trying to keep the bitterness out of his voice. "I'm here. Are you close?" Heavy breathing echoed over the line, and a steady pounding as if running upstairs.

"Almost there. Fifth floor, right? The elevator is broken. Why is everything broken today?" She mumbled the last sentence, and Parker wondered what she meant.

"It worked for me. Maybe they're fixing something on it?" He heard a click and saw that she'd ended the call.

Not much longer, and he saw her come around the corner. He raised his hand to his mouth, trying to cover any reactions to her disheveled appearance. With mud smeared down one side of her face and her hair either sticking outwards or to the mud, his heart beat a little faster.

"What time is my interview?" She looked at him as if finally registering that he was there. "What are you doing here? Did I tell you about this?"

Parker shook his head. "No, you didn't. They called me

yesterday and asked me to come in for some interview. Is that why you're here?"

Exasperated, Meg put her hand on her hip and rolled her eyes. "They called me about some segment on my business. I was going to say something last night, but I completely forgot." Her eyes darted around the hallway. "What's the schedule, do you know?"

"There was a lady looking for the both of us back in there." He pointed to the large double doors behind her.

"Oh, here's a bathroom. Give me one, okay, maybe two minutes to make myself presentable before we see anyone else." She disappeared into the ladies bathroom, and Parker looked down at his watch. Already five minutes late, they were lucky it wasn't a live show.

Thinking he'd be standing out there forever, she emerged only three minutes later, and he almost had to pick his mouth up off the floor. She'd washed off the mud and pulled her hair into an elegant side ponytail. She also changed her shirt, and shoes, the same black glittery high-heeled ones she'd worn to dinner the other night.

"Ready?"

"After the day I've had, I don't even know." She brushed her hair back over her shoulder and slung the large bag over her shoulder.

The woman with the curly, black hair looked annoyed as they finally found her. "You're late." She gave them a look as if her anger could turn back the clock.

"But we're here, so tell us where to go." The edge to Meg's voice caused the woman to deepen her frown. Parker hadn't thought it possible, but there it was, lines and puckering of lips. He looked back at Meg and couldn't help but smile as he watched her stare down the other woman.

Finally relenting, the woman disappeared behind a wall

and reemerged, handing them both microphone packs. "Put these on. You'll go on after this segment. Susie—"

"I'm sorry, we're going on together?" Meg pointed at Parker.

"That can't be right. The woman who called said it was a segment on—"

"On your relationship with Miss Austen."

Parker shook his head. "No, it was about—I"

"I'm sorry. We don't have time for this." The woman looked down at her clipboard. "The segment will be about ten minutes long, so just smile and when you're speaking, look at Susie. You want to make it more of a conversational piece, so please, don't stare at the camera."

Meg ran her fingers over her hair and pulled out some lipstick. She put it on without a mirror and had just put the lipstick away when Parker noticed a small smear below her bottom lip.

"Here, let me help you with that." He swiped his thumb, taking with it the wayward lipstick. They stood close together, eyes staring at one another. If he thought it were possible, there would have been a bolt of electricity jumping back and forth between them.

"Go sit down on the stage. We need to get back on schedule." The woman practically pushed them to two upholstered armchairs sitting at an angle with another one.

As a woman stepped onto the set, he could tell by her expression he was in for a long ten minutes. Wearing a tight red dress that hugged too much around the chest, she gave him a doe-eyed look. She bent to shake his hand, exaggerating the motion to show off her cleavage and for some reason, an image of Courtney popped into his mind.

She merely nodded to Meg, who chewed on something as her jaw flexed.

"I'm Susie Somerset, host of the show. Thanks for coming

out today." She sat straight up, one leg crossed over the other while she scanned several papers in her lap. She looked up moments later and said, "What an interesting story we have today. I can't wait to get all the details. Do you watch the show, Parker?"

"I think I heard my stepmother mention it a time or two, but I've never seen it." Parker kept his face neutral, already feeling the awkwardness of being there.

Susie shot him an overeager smile. "Nothing better than experiencing it firsthand then." Parker turned to Meg, her eyes shooting daggers at Susie. This should be fun.

The set went quiet, and the camera in front of them turned on, the red light above signaling action. Parker watched the monitor as several words floated up, and Susie read them, almost word for word. After a few moments, he remembered the directions of the producer and had to tear his eyes away. Conversational. Relaxed.

"Today's guests come sharing an interesting story. Meg Austen is the owner of Love, Austen, a matchmaking company here in Boston. Sitting next to her is the attractive Parker Matthews, a divorce attorney for Matthews, Brooks, and Park Law Firm."

Looking away from the camera, Susie smiled at him. "Thanks for being with us today."

After exchanging hellos, Susie turned to Meg. "Meg, why don't you tell us a little about your business and how you came up with the idea."

"Of course. It started as a term project for my psych class. We had to come up with something unique based on several criteria. My friend and I have always loved watching Jane Austen films, and I had the idea to create a way for others to find love."

Meg smiled, her nerves barely visible as she tucked a stray piece of hair behind her ear. "After a semester of research and collecting data, I created the system we use now to find the closest match possible for our clients. Over the past few years, it's grown from a small operation in my one-bedroom apartment, to an office building and several success stories."

"Where is your business located?" Susie looked down at her paper after asking the question. Meg shifted in her seat, looking uncomfortable.

She cleared her throat and said, "We moved into a building down on Beacon Street, two buildings east of Trader Joe's. So, if you're in Boston, come see us. If not, we're working on an app for the business which we hope to launch next year."

"Awesome," Susie said the word without enthusiasm and turned to Parker, her tone changing to a silky, soothing one. "Welcome, Parker. So, it sounds like you two are an item. When did all this happen?"

Parker's chest tightened. Numbers and dates escaped him as his mind went blank. He turned to Meg who just smiled at him.

"It's been a few weeks. We met at the wedding of mutual friends." Meg's smile brightened her voice, and Susie didn't so much as look at her.

"I have to say we've been following you for the past two years, and it's somewhat surprising that you finally picked one woman to be with. What is it about her that keeps you around?" Parker had to blink as the words from Susie seemed like a purr.

He turned to look at Meg. They smiled at each other, and he reached out, grabbing her hand. He could feel her relax and hoped he wouldn't mess up.

"She's someone I wish I'd met years ago. Every day has been an adventure so far, and there's so much to love about her. She's intelligent, funny, beautiful. I could go on, but I know the show is only so long." He laughed and heard laughter around the studio.

Susie's face signaled boredom as she asked, "You met at a wedding. Did you dance and exchange numbers? Our viewers want to know."

Or she wants to know.

Parker chuckled, trying to lessen the uneasiness in his stomach. "She was the maid of honor, and I was a guest of the groom. She liked me so much she sort of fell into my arms." Meg stiffened, and she gave him a wide-eyed look he couldn't read.

"Well, that's all the time we have, but thank you both for coming by." Susie shook their hands and then read the few words on the screen before the show went to break.

She looked at Parker and said, "What are you doing later? I know this great place that serves fun drinks."

Parker wasn't sure what to say and opened his mouth, trying to think of the best let down. Before he could get anything out, Meg said it for him.

"Are you serious right now? You just interviewed us as a couple, and you're hitting on him?" She raised her fists and let out a disgusted breath.

As she pushed between Susie and Parker, he saw her elbow the host in the rib. She picked up her bag and sprinted to the exit.

Looking over at Susie, who looked like she was trying to catch her breath, he said, "I'm flattered, but she's right. We're together. Thanks for the interview."

arker took off after Meg, surprised at how fast she could walk when she was angry. When he caught up to her, she had her head down, looking at her phone.

"Hey! You okay? What happened in there?" When she looked up, he realized it was the wrong thing to ask.

"What happened in there? Let me flaunt myself to a guy who's taken and then only address him because why would a guy like you go out with a girl like me?" She let out a short yell.

After a moment, she turned to him. "I'm fine. This whole fake relationship thing is little more than I thought it would be. Besides, with everything going on at the office, I'm just a little frazzled. So much for plugging the gala." She stood there for a minute, tapping her foot.

She'd said the words as fast as spilling a glass of milk, and he took a minute to catch up. He knew better than to smile as she imitated Susie's posture and actions with perfection, but inside, he could feel his abs tighten from the laughter. "Yeah, you're right. Was that supposed to happen?"

Meg rolled her eyes. "Who knows?" The elevator doors opened, and they walked inside.

Under her breath, she said, "What I wouldn't give to restart this day."

Parker reached over and put his arm around her shoulder, pulling her closer. He could feel resistance in the beginning, but she finally put her arms around his waist, her head leaning into his chest as she sobbed. He stroked her hair, amazed that it was still soft after all she'd been through. Wait, what had she been through?

"What did you mean, 'everything going on at the office?'" All too soon, the doors opened, and a few people stood waiting to enter, staring at them.

She lifted her head and pulled away, but he kept his arm on her side, pulling her through the doors and past the people. A bench was just outside the main doors, and he sat her down on it.

Leaning against him, she cried for several minutes, and Parker worked to be sympathetic. It was harder than he thought it would be as her face scrunched up, her eyes puffy. The red splotches on her face reminded him of a skin disease. He'd never been good with crying, and he just hoped he didn't make things worse while trying to help.

When she finally calmed down and sat up, she dug into her big shoulder bag, wiping under her eyes with her fingers and dabbing at her face with a tissue.

"I'm so sorry. It's been like two years since I last cried, this hard anyway, and I'm sorry you had to be here to witness the ugly-crying face."

"You look fine. It's not ugly, you just look like you're allergic to bees and got stung."

Frowning, she punched him in the shoulder, and Parker was surprised that it hurt. Not much, but more than he expected.

Sniffling, she said, "On my way here, I got a call that the office had been flooded. I went to check it out, then the thing with the train getting stuck. My only bright spot was Tiffany saying only two invitations for the gala came back to sender today."

He smiled, tucking some of her blond hair behind her ear. "Should we go check out your office?"

"You don't have to go to work?"

"I wasn't sure how long this whole interview would take. Besides, it's lunchtime anyway. I'll drive, and we can grab some food later."

They both stood, and the front doors opened. The producer came running out, waving an envelope at the two of them. Parker took it from her, and the woman ran inside without a word.

Meg giggled. "That was odd."

"Yeah, it was." He slid his finger through the back of the envelope and pulled out a small note.

Thanks for helping the show. I'll be watching! Cherice

Shaking his head, he handed Meg the note. As she read it, he looked inside to find a gift certificate to The Capital Grille.

"Looks like we know why we were on the show. I should've connected this to Cherice. Bart said a few months ago, how she'd been helping one of the local channels. I didn't realize this was one of those shows."

Meg smiled. "Well, at least we get a good dinner out of it."

"I finally feel like I'm doing something to help you. Being on the show together is a plus with your investors. Maybe we should send an anonymous tape to them just to make sure they saw us on there."

"I hadn't even thought about that. That could be a good idea. I haven't heard from them in over a week, and I'm starting to worry." Meg bit her bottom lip as she looked down the street. At what, he wasn't sure.

"You told them about the gala though, right?" Parker focused on tucking the card back into the envelope.

Meg nodded, turning her attention back to him. "Yeah, so they'll be there for sure. I just need to get through the next week and see how everything turns out."

Part of Parker couldn't wait for that moment, hoping they would be able to keep this relationship going long after. Now he just needed to figure out if Meg's outburst with Susie was because she felt something for him, or if the stress was getting to her.

CHAPTER 25

Grabbing sandwiches at a local deli, they made their way over to the office. Meg was too keyed up to eat, running into the office after they parked.

"Hi George. Any word on the result?" As she glanced around, she was grateful to see only a thin sheen of water on the multicolored carpet.

"It looks like most of it is covered by the other insurance agency. We caught it before it went up too far on the wall. We'll just have to replace some trim in the bathroom and along the stairs. And then just air out the carpets. I've been working to remove most of the water, and the restoration guys took your furniture to make sure it doesn't get worse."

Hope blossomed in her chest. "So, I won't have to move out?"

George shook his head, and Meg jumped up to give him a hug. When she let go, she turned, wrapping her arms around Parker.

"This day is looking up by the minute. Now, if I can just find the decorations for the gala, all the stress will be gone from my life."

"If you don't need to do anything here, why don't we go shopping for whatever you need?"

Meg studied his face, trying to decide if he was serious.

Waving her hand in front of him, she said, "Are you feeling all right? Watching *Emma*, then reading *Emma*, and now you want to help me shop for decorations. Don't you have some work to do to get that *big partnership*?" She exaggerated the last two words, bringing a smile to his face.

"All the work I have to do will still be there when we finish. Besides, if I can help make you smile after all that's happened today, I'm in."

And there went her heart, crashing into her ribs. She hoped they could handle it.

"Okay, but let's take the train." Not that her last experience with it was that great, but it would be easier than finding parking for his car at every stop.

She saw his head cock to the side. "What if we find things we want to buy? How will we carry them back here?" The confusion on his face made her smile.

They walked out the door. "Ah, my young apprentice. You will learn the ways of shopping from me." She tried to continue with the strange voice, but they both laughed too much. "Basically, I like to visit stores and make notes of what I think would be good. After I've seen all the options, or the ones I have time for, I get them ordered, and they deliver it to the event center."

"Okay, so do you have a theme? I've never really planned a party before, so my knowledge comes from reality TV shows." The innocent look on his face made Meg want to close the distance and kiss him.

Focus. Investors coming to the gala.

"I'm hoping to recreate a Regency ball. Period attire is optional, but formal dress is required for everyone."

"You said you'd ordered some decorations before, but they wouldn't arrive in time?"

Meg nodded, tapping her pointer finger over her lips. "Yes, but now that I think about it, it's best those didn't come. They would have been too modern for the look we're going for."

After going through three shops and finding little things that could add to the picture she had in her mind, Meg felt the frustration web inside her stomach. How would she find all she needed for the party on such short notice?

Parker raised a finger and said, "I've got it. You should have Jane Austen quotes about love on all the tables."

"I should have thought of that. It's brilliant." Ideas marched through her mind. "We could get the large, glass bowls from that last place and have daisies floating on water for a centerpiece. Next to it, a quote in calligraphy. We'll need some sort of table runner or decorative napkin underneath it." She hugged him again, reaching up on tiptoe to give him a kiss on the cheek.

"Let me call Tiffany and have her order the flowers and a few other things." As she held the phone to her ear, she rocked back and forth, watching Parker take in the display of one of the windows as she did so.

If anything, he was the best luck she had. Finding her a caterer and helping her figure out the start of the decorations. But would her luck hold after the month was out?

After Susie's interview earlier, Meg wasn't sure she had a flicker of a chance to keep him around forever.

*P*arker rubbed his fingers in a circular motion along his temples, wishing the pounding would subside. He'd been staring at the same sheet of paper for the past ten minutes and still couldn't make heads or tails of it.

He kept thinking about the look on Meg's face as he dropped her off the night before, buzzing about the décor, and it eased his mind.

"She's good for you." Bart walked in, slipping into his customary chair in front of Parker's desk.

Yes, she is. Parker smiled, unsure how to answer the comment aloud. Sometimes the best way was to ignore it.

"What can I do for you, boss?" He leaned back in his swivel chair, tapping a pen in his hand.

"I need you to take over two of my cases for the next week. Our new hire comes Monday, and I'd like you to show her around. It's my anniversary tomorrow, and we're going on a cruise for a few days."

"You never mentioned this before. Which two cases?"

"Salvatore and O'Donnell."

Parker felt all the air rush out of him. Those were the two biggest cases at their law firm right now and if anything went wrong, he'd be disqualified from partner. But as he looked at a picture of him and Meg sitting on his desk, the two of them laughing in one of the swan boats from their day out, he wondered if that would be the worst thing to happen to him.

"I'll do it. I didn't know we had a new hire." He focused on Bart, trying to remember any news he might have forgotten.

"She's moving here from Illinois, taking over for Stacy, who won't be coming back after maternity leave." Clapping Parker on the back, Bart said, "Thanks for doing that for me. By the way, you and Meg did a great job on that show yesterday."

Parker pretended to frown. "Tell Cherice she'd better watch her back. I'll have to come up with something good to get her back."

"I'd love to see you try. The show was my idea."

"What?"

Bart grinned, irritation welling up in Parker's throat. "I wanted to see how you'd react to some public attention on your relationship. Just one of the tests for partner."

"Did you have Susie ask me out?"

With a quick shake of the head, Bart started to laugh. "No, but from the look on your face, I'm sure that went over well. How'd Meg take it?"

"Not well at first. She'd had some problems with flooding at her office in the morning, so it just added to the tension."

Bart stood, walking to the doorway. "Okay, I'll have the files sent over so you can get started."

"What did you think about us on the show?" Parker's curiosity couldn't be contained any longer. Sure, it might have had bearing on his appointment to partner, but he was more curious for an outsider's opinion on Meg's feelings for him.

The corner of Bart's mouth turned up. "She's one of the good ones, Parker. That's why I think you need to keep her around, even if you get the partnership."

Ten minutes later, fifteen boxes of files were stuffed into the open space in his office. Parker knew he was in trouble. How would he be able to go through these before their scheduled meetings? He pulled out several items and papers from a box and realized none of it had been categorized.

Meg. Maybe she'd have a game plan on categorizing all this stuff.

Any chance you could help me out tonight?

Parker's thumb hesitated over the send button, nervous. Why did it feel like he was asking her out on a date? He finally pushed it, and her response came through within a few seconds, surprising him.

Sure. What time?

Does seven work?

Yep. I'll be close to the Common. Where should we meet?

Parker paused, his eyes going over the boxes again.

I'll have everything taken to my apartment. I was thinking maybe we could get some takeout while we go over all the information. That all right?

The seconds waiting for her response seemed like an eternity. He finally had to put his phone on the desk to keep the nervous energy down.

Sounds great. I'll pick up something on my way over. Will you text me your address?

As he sent it from his desk at work, he tried to picture the state of his apartment. He'd left in a rush that morning, and it had been a few weeks since he'd cleaned up. Looking at his watch now, he saw it was almost three o'clock.

He still had things to go over, but he knew he wouldn't be

able to concentrate on anything until he'd cleaned up. But he'd have to get a truck to take all the boxes over to his apartment. He picked up his desk phone and dialed, making the arrangements with the firm courier.

When he arrived at his apartment, he realized he'd made the right choice. If Meg was coming over, he had to make sure she didn't gag as soon as she walked into the bathroom, if she had to go.

Throwing on his old college t-shirt and a pair of gym shorts, he pulled out a box of cleaning supplies and turned on his favorite playlist. Tackling the bathroom first, he scrubbed, wiped, and swept, moving on to each room in his two-bedroom apartment. He'd had to work around the boxes, which had been delivered around five o'clock.

When the doorbell rang, Parker looked up to see that it was already seven. Lifting his arm, he smelled his armpits and choked. He'd have to do something about that. The last thing he wanted to do was repel Meg with his stench.

He shoved the cleaning supplies back under the sink and walked over to the door. Opening it, he smiled as Meg stood there with a large pizza and a paper bag on top. Her hair was up, but several pieces had fallen out, framing her face.

"You found me."

"It wasn't too bad. Even though you give me a hard time about my directional skills." She tipped her chin up, looking like she'd won some unspoken contest.

"I only moved your arm on our adventure. I've never given you a hard time about it." He tried to paste on a serious expression. "Did you use your phone?"

She scrunched her nose and pursed her lips at the comment, causing Parker to laugh. "Maybe. Can I come in?"

"Oh, yeah, sorry. Put the food there on the counter and make yourself at home. I'm just going to take a quick shower, and then we can get started."

She took off her purse, and he laughed at her shirt that said, 'Readers gonna read.' When he made a comment on it, she said, "Well, from the look of all these boxes, that's what we'll be doing tonight."

"That it is." He left her on the sofa and practically ran to the bathroom, anxious to get back to her.

eg looked around the room, taking it in. She'd heard Beacon Hill was one of the upper-class areas to live and while this apartment was nice, she wondered if it was worth the price he had to pay for rent.

"What do I know?" she muttered to herself. "I've lived in the same room for the last six years. Anywhere else will be more expensive, especially if it's in the city."

It looked like a single male lived here, for sure. The living area held a leather sectional with a glass coffee table in front. A large flat-screen TV hung from the wall, and dark bookshelves sat on each side. The shelves held law books on one side, with several fantasy and thriller books on the other. He'd bought not only *Emma*, but all the other Jane Austen books sat neatly placed next to each other. He was taking this fake boyfriend thing to a whole other level. Or was he?

There were only a few pictures, one that looked like Parker when he was five or six. He was holding up a large fish and next to him stood a boy at least a head shorter. She couldn't remember how she knew he had a brother, but she thought of Tiffany's request.

Another picture showed Parker dressed in graduation robes, standing next to an older Parker with a mustache.

"That's my dad," Parker said from behind her. She jumped and turned to face him. He moved his hand back and forth through his short hair, and droplets of water sprayed out behind him. Dressed in a pair of basketball shorts and a t-shirt, Meg had to smile as she remembered their conversation about relaxing.

"Was it from graduation?"

"Yeah, law school. It was the happiest I've ever seen him." Parker moved next to Meg, his shoulder right behind her. She could smell the clean, manly scent on him. She turned to study his face as he looked closer at the picture.

"Were you close with him?"

"Yes," he said as he put the picture back down and turned his head, "and no. We had our moments, but he was always there, unlike my mother."

"Is that your brother?" She pointed to the picture of the fish, and he nodded.

After what seemed like forever, he said, "He died about a year after that picture. Leukemia."

"Oh, Parker. I'm so sorry. Why didn't you tell me?"

He looked at her, a sad smile forming. "I haven't thought about it in so long. We were so young, I only remember bits and pieces of life with him."

They stared at each other, and Meg could feel the tension pulling her closer to him. Leaning in, she gave him a hug, resting her head on his chest for a few beats. When she pulled back, she looked at his lips again and found that he was leaning forward.

His lips touched hers gently, and the familiar tingle flared up from the times she'd kissed him before. He pulled back a second, looking into her eyes. She breathed in his soap and went on tiptoe to kiss him back.

She wrapped her arms around his neck, and he pulled her in tighter, his arms moving around her waist. His touch was soft along the small of her back and if she could stop time right there, with her lips on his, she would.

Her mind seemed clouded at first, until it showed her an image of Susie and a picture of Parker's ex-girlfriend. She'd looked her up, curious as to his type. All for the sake of her business of course. Their gorgeous, olive-skinned complexions were the opposite of her Irish skin. Doubt washed over her. Was he kissing her because she was convenient?

She drew back, pulling him with her. His eyes were still closed, lips puckered, waiting for hers to return to him.

"I'm so sorry. Are you okay?" She saw panic wash over his features, and she smiled, hoping it would reassure him.

Clearing her throat, she said, "Where's your bathroom? We should get started on all these boxes." It sounded odd, even to her, but she didn't know how to address the sparks between them. As much as the doubt bugged her, she didn't want to ruin the moment any further.

"Down that hall, and to the right. I'll get us some plates for the pizza."

Shutting the door, Meg leaned up against it, breathing heavier than normal. The smell of him was even stronger in the bathroom as steam still fogged up the corners of the mirror. And the feel of his lips on hers, the way his arms held her.

What was she doing? Had she been single for too long and at the first interest of a guy, she was going along with it?

She wiped underneath her eyes and shook her head. Parker was a good guy, and she wouldn't mind kissing him every day for the rest of her life. The thought scared her. What if he got sick? Or he got in an accident? Could she survive knowing she'd lost her heart along with him?

The biggest question was, did he have feelings for her?

Until she knew for sure, she couldn't risk giving him all her heart.

Opening the door, her mind buzzed with warnings. Walking into the front room, she avoided his eyes and said, "I'm so sorry. There's been an emergency, and I have to go. I feel terrible I can't help you tonight. Will you be okay?"

Worry etched itself into his face. "Are you sure? Do you want me to drive you there, wherever it is?"

Shaking her head, Meg said, "No. I'll be fine. I'm sorry to bail, it's just this thing needs to be fixed now."

Little did he know it was her, and there was no fix.

He waved her off and walked behind her to the door. She pulled it open, and he said, "Be safe."

Leaning over, he gave her a lingering kiss, and Meg's resolve weakened. She gave him a small smile, grabbing her purse, and walked out the door.

Tears splashed down her face even before she made it to the stairs. He was almost perfect. There was no way she could stop herself from being hurt by him. Their fake relationship had gone too far. Maybe it was time to end it and see where things stood.

CHAPTER 28

*P*arker had seen the walls go up after she'd come out of the bathroom, and he knew there was no going back for him. He was head over heels for her, and it was difficult to concentrate on his work over the next few days.

He'd spent the weekend holed up in his apartment, reading through as much of the information as he needed to, falling asleep at his desk more than once. The information was boring and when he thought about the couple's beginning and their future, a weight pushed down on his chest, making it hard to breathe.

It reminded him of his parents' divorce.

How long can I continue to do this?

The thought caught him off guard. Do what? Find ways to break up marriages by focusing on the numbers, the assets, the fairness. Sifting through lies and manipulation in some cases. Or as Meg would say, be the ultimate Dream Killer of Love.

Every time he picked up his phone to call or text her, he pictured the glazed look she'd plastered over her face as she practically ran from his apartment. He knew he'd have to do something to break through her fear.

When he saw her name pop up on his phone Monday morning, he had to count to three before he answered it, not wanting to scare her away any more by seeming desperate.

"Hey, Meg. How are things going?" *Great start. Now she'll just think you're friends.*

He heard her clear her throat on the other end. "Good. The carpet is all dry, and our furniture should be ready in the next few days, so I'm back in the office, trying to match people from the, well, a couple of categories. I was calling because I forgot to tell you the details for the gala on Saturday."

"Of course. What time and where should I meet you? Can I pick you up?"

There was a slight hesitation before she finally spoke again. "It starts at six, and I'll probably be there earlier, so I can make sure everything will go according to plan. Would you mind meeting me there?"

"Yeah, I guess I can do that." What he really wanted to say was something a lot more romantic but couldn't think of just yet. "What do I need to wear?"

"A suit or a tux, whatever you feel like wearing."

"Okay, sounds good." He hung up the phone, his mind spinning with ideas. She liked him. It wasn't like he'd been the only one kissing, especially since he'd pulled back, and she kissed him again. And when she'd gone a little crazy after the talk show host's invitation for drinks. Was he reading too much into it?

The gala. He'd tell her how he felt then and hope they could change their fake relationship into a real one.

* * *

MEG STARED at the phone a few seconds after the call disconnected. Her stomach was doing an all-out tumbling routine while her brain was trying to convince it to do anything else. As much as she wanted to, she couldn't get his lips out of her mind. What was it about him that made her feel so crazy?

It wasn't like she hadn't kissed guys before, but the moment her lips touched his, she felt like she'd been through a desert, and his lips were the source of water.

Okay, that analogy was actually rather good. Why did it have to be about Parker though?

She frowned just as Tiffany walked in the door.

"What's with the frown? Did something else go wrong with the gala? Did the venue catch on fire? Ever since that happened with Hampshire House for Lily's wedding, I have nightmares it will happen for the gala."

Meg squeezed her eyes shut. "No word about the reception hall, but now I'll be worried about it until Saturday." She needed to be calm, collected, and focused. "Just things with Parker have been a little off."

Instead of the sad look she was hoping for, Tiffany gave her a scalding one. "Are you sure things are feeling 'off' or are you trying to run away?"

Shame burned her cheeks. Was that true?

Taking a seat, Tiffany crossed her feet and set them on Meg's desk. "Start from the beginning. What happened?"

Meg explained the details about helping him go over case files. After she described the kisses and her quick departure, Tiffany rolled her eyes.

"Permission to speak as a friend instead of an employee?" Meg didn't like the dread sinking like a rock into the sea of her stomach.

"Sure."

Tiffany leaned forward, staring right into Meg's eyes. "You *like* like him. Admit it!"

"I… well, there are some feelings there. Why would I have started dating him if I didn't like him?"

"What made you run from his apartment?"

Meg stared at the corner of the office, trying to keep the tears at bay. Why was she so emotional all of a sudden? She'd been moving along just fine before she met Parker. Now, she was just another girl who wore her emotions on her sleeve.

"The thought that if I fall in love with him and something happens, like he dies or decides he doesn't want to be with me anymore. I looked up his ex-girlfriend, and she's gorgeous. What if he goes back to her? I just don't know if I could bounce back from that."

"You did with Steve. You're a mostly functioning adult. Besides, he said he hasn't seen her in what? Three years? What makes you think that will happen?"

Meg picked up a paper clip and flicked it. Tiffany dodged it with a smile. "What do you mean, 'mostly functioning adult?'"

"You won't let yourself feel. So, let's make a plan. What did you do to get over Steve?"

As details filtered to her mind that she'd been blocking for so long, Meg bit her lip hard enough she reached up to see if there was blood.

"It wasn't that hard to get over him, honestly. I mean, no one wants to find out the guy she's with is cheating on her. But the pain faded faster than I thought it would. He had so many quirks, I knew things would never work out."

"What's different about Parker?"

"I've never felt emotions this intense. What if he breaks my heart?"

Tiffany walked around the desk and pulled Meg up into a hug. "You have so many people cheering you on. Lily, Ben, me. Some of your favorite clients. We would all be here to put you back together. But from how that man looks at you, I don't think it will happen."

The phone rang out in the lobby, and Tiffany pulled back, gave Meg a knowing smile, and walked out to answer it.

Was it possible this relationship could work? As much as she hoped Tiffany was right, her assistant had only met him once, and that was before the sparks flew like firecrackers.

Now, the biggest question remained. Was he worth the leap?

CHAPTER 29

*M*eg woke up with the birds on Saturday morning. Thinking back, she couldn't distinguish one day from another as the past week had been a whirlwind of matching and preparations.

Since this was a company party of sorts, she liked to get as many of the matches set up, so they had time to mingle and dance while there. She thought of it as a gift for the first date since no one had to plan anything. Thirty-six new people matched in the past week. That was more than the last two months combined.

After the influx of new clients from the talk show, she and Tiffany implemented the newer methods, which relied heavily on references. At times, she wanted to throw the phone out the window, but she learned important characteristics faster, already saving her valuable time.

She hadn't gone to bed until after midnight the night before. Tiffany and a few others she'd recruited helped decorate the hall they were using for the gala. She'd had to settle for simple, as many of the ideas she'd had would have taken way more time than she had. But the lengths of tulle, the dozens of electric candles, and the layout of the centerpieces on the tables made it look elegant.

The deep tone of Parker's voice echoed in her head. They'd talked on the phone the night before when she'd asked him if he wanted to help again. Regret tinged his voice when he said he couldn't make it. He was only halfway through the boxes and with court appearances for them Monday morning, he wouldn't have time to come.

They had chatted a bit more, the conversation flowing easier than it had in days, and Meg felt lighter than she had in a while once they hung up.

Now, after running errands all morning, she was back at the reception hall, sweeping the main floor from the dust and pieces of paper that had fallen while they decorated.

"What are you still doing here? You should be at home getting ready." Tiffany's mom voice grated on Meg, and she gave the girl a fake smile.

"This has to be perfect. The growth and future of our company depends on this going well."

Tiffany put her hands on Meg's shoulders and turned her towards the exit, gently pushing as they walked along.

"It looks perfect now. But you are the face of the company and if you don't look perfect, that could say something to the investors."

From the look on Tiffany's face, Meg knew she didn't mean it, but it struck a chord anyway.

"My dress is at the office. I'll just go there."

"Nope," was Tiffany's sassy reply. Meg wanted to punch her. "I brought it here. One of our hair girls will get you all pretty. You can't have a Jane Austen gala without a little relaxation time."

Some annoyance melted away as Meg realized she

wouldn't have to ride public transportation, rush to get ready, and then jump back on to get back to the hall. She stepped forward and covered Tiffany in a hug. Maybe she should look into buying a car after this.

"Thank you so much. I know I've been a little off lately, but thanks for putting up with me."

"Are you kidding? I'm just trying to get some time off. Or a raise even." Tiffany winked at her.

"Well, remind me next week that we need to talk about more benefits for you. Saving my sanity has its perks."

Meg walked back to the designated makeover room and as the girl pulled and twisted her hair, Meg fell into a trance. Her eyes closed for what seemed like a few minutes but when she opened them again, her hair and makeup were almost complete.

Soft curls pinned near the crown of her head, and she saw miniature pearls stuck every few inches. Two small ringlets hung on the sides of her face and as she stared, she had to blink several times to recognize herself.

"Wow! You all do such an amazing job." She turned, to see another gal getting her hair done and found her own hair-dresser had moved on to the next. "I'm so sorry I fell asleep. It'll be nice when this is all over."

"I figured you needed some rest," Olivia said, talking around several bobby pins between her lips. "Hopefully, it was enough to help you have a fantastic night." Her hands moved with ease through the client's hair, parting and pinning in quick succession.

"Have you had enough business today?" As part of the full-package program, clients received the makeovers as part of their fee. But she'd let all the guests know they could come and enjoy the day. They just paid for the services like a normal salon.

"We had to take shifts for lunch." The girl laughed, wrapping hair around a curling iron. "I'm game for helping out any time you have one of these events though. We've all made more today than all last week."

Meg smiled. That was what she was hoping for. Nothing like helping other people while working on her own business.

Looking at her phone, she saw there were only ten minutes before the gala would officially start. The calm she'd felt moments before fled, a gnawing panic taking its place.

"Did Tiffany bring a dress in here earlier? She said she brought it from our office."

One of the other hairdressers pointed to the far wall.

Because of the flooding, Meg had doled out the dresses earlier than normal so that the ladies could store them at their houses a couple of days before the gala. She'd taken the one remaining dress in her size, an empire-waisted pink dress, cap-sleeved with several beads sewn into the bodice.

Rushing to get into it, she hurried out into the lobby and found several guests already in the ballroom. The ballet flats she'd chosen for the night already felt more comfortable than heels, and she was sure her feet would appreciate it by the end of the night.

Greeting as many as she could, her eyes darted back and forth looking for Tiffany. Finally locating her assistant, who'd changed into a mint dress, Meg rushed to her, trying to stay composed.

"Is everything okay? Did the caterer show up? Are all the plates and everything set out?"

Tiffany grinned. "And everything is ready. Lexi Sarmiento arrived an hour and a half ago, and things smelled delicious when I left the kitchen just now. The string quartet is all set up in the ballroom. For now, all you have to do is flash those pearly whites as you greet people."

"Really?" It felt like a large boulder had moved off her chest, and she could finally breathe. "When this is over, we need to hire a few other employees, and we'll have a chat about you managing them or something." If tonight went well, they'd need the extra help, and Tiffany had beyond earned it.

*P*arker arrived thirty minutes early and went in search of Meg. After long hours of staring at briefs and every paper the O'Donnells had saved during their thirty-four-year marriage, he was glad to get out of his apartment.

He still felt guilty for turning down Meg's request to help decorate, but at least she seemed to have relaxed, and he hoped he could find a moment to tell her how he felt. Besides, he still had a part to play, and he figured he better be there in case the investors showed up early.

Walking in the door, he grinned from ear to ear at the sight of the décor. At a normal function, he wouldn't have given it a second thought but as he took in the elegant garlands swinging from one end of the room to the other, it made him think of their day shopping.

The floating daisies sat upon a small stack of what looked like antique books on each table. Next to that were small notes in beautiful script, quotes on love from Jane Austen herself.

Several other people milled about the entrance, friends greeting other friends dressed in traditional dresses or tuxes.

Parker pulled at the lapels on his coat. It had taken longer than he wanted but with the help of a friend, he'd found an ensemble like what some men wore in the Jane Austen films. He'd just been grateful they could have it ready for him today since he'd thought of it so late.

Making it through the door, he saw Meg greeting several people in front of him. He found her attractive on a normal day, and today was no exception with her hair up. The pink dress she wore was elegant, and it brightened her complexion.

She caught his eye as she greeted the couple in front of him and smiled, the surprise fading quickly. Once it was his turn, he hugged her and kissed her on the lips, unable to resist being so close to her without it. He wanted to linger but knew the line was only growing behind him. She drew back, eyes wide, and he winked at her.

"You never know who's watching." He gave her a devious smile, all the while wishing he could confess the real reason he'd kissed her.

As she took in his appearance, he saw glee in her eyes as she bounced on her toes. "Where did you find this outfit? I need more of these for the guys."

"I have my ways. But I can definitely give you my contact." He turned to stand beside her. "Is there anything else I need to do? Do you want me to stand here or help somewhere else?"

She bit her lower lip. The motion made him wish they were alone so he could kiss her again. "Stay here. I've been a little off today, and it will be good to have you here." She paused a moment and then finished too quickly, "In case the investors get here."

The words felt like a stab to the heart, but there was a

pause in there. And he'd made the comment about never knowing who's watching. Why had he said that? Nothing like sending the wrong signals.

He leaned over and whispered into her ear, "Do you know what these investors look like?"

"Only one. But they said they'd be sending several." She leaned in as she whispered it, and her orange blossom scent filled his senses. "I want to check on the kitchen before it gets too late. Walk with me."

He liked the simple command in her voice. *To the ends of the earth.*

Parker shook his head. He could get as mushy as he wanted when this thing was all over. For now, he had a part to play, and he would do it as well as he could.

"That should be easy, right? Just look for the people you don't know?" It was strange to hear only his boots on the wooden floor and when he looked down, he found Meg wearing soft shoes that looked almost like slippers. "No heels tonight, huh?" One side of his mouth curled, and she gave him a mischievous grin.

"It's best if I avoid any slipping and tripping tonight, even if you're here to save me." He noted the laughter in her eyes, and he recalled the two times he'd caught her from crashing into the ground.

"But I don't mind it." He couldn't help it. His heart skipped when she flashed him a grin.

Meg picked up her dress with her hands and seemed to float across the floor. "As far as strangers for the gala, I wish it were that easy to pick out the investors. We do the gala as a fun night out for our clients and former clients, but each of them can bring an extra guest. This is our second year doing the gala and last year, we received several new clients from those referrals."

Parker tried to make his face look approving. "That's a

great idea. But I can see how that would make it hard to weed out the investors."

They pushed into the kitchen, and Parker breathed in the smell of garlic and onions. Seeing a familiar face, he walked forward and said, "Lexi!"

The short girl turned to look at him, flour dusting one side of her cheek. "Hey, Parker! Thanks again for getting me this gig. Maybe one day I'll have my own restaurant."

Meg stood beside him. "Are you kidding? With the way these plates look and how it smells in here, you'll have a place in no time." She bent forward, looking at the intricate dessert tray. "What are these?"

"Tres leches cake, picarones, which is a Peruvian doughnut, and pastelitos, which is an Argentine pastry. It's nice to get out of the family kitchen and create my own masterpieces. I know this is more of a British occasion with the theme and all, but I wanted to give them something different for dessert."

"I love the idea, and I can't wait to try them." She leaned forward, speaking in a loud whisper, "Just another reason I love the Regency era: the dresses aren't form-fitting, and I can try them all."

The two girls shared a wink, and Parker rolled his lips in, trying to stay neutral. It seemed a lot harder to do that now. He was head over heels in love with Meg. The biggest question was if she would return his feelings once all the pressure of the investors died down?

"Can I just say thank you one more time?" she said as they walked back to the dining room.

"For what?" He caught her swinging arm and laced his fingers with hers, the shockwave of nerves firing, making him wonder how he'd been so lucky to meet her.

She pointed towards the kitchen with the other hand. "For that in there. For keeping me somewhat sane with the decorations and the food. I'd say this place would be a mess without your help." Her eyes connected with his and before he knew it consciously, he leaned forward, pressing his lips to hers.

A bell sounded from a nearby clocktower, and they broke apart. Six o'clock.

"Are you ready for this?"

"As ready as I'm going to be. Let's get back out there so we can greet the guests." He noted the pink tinge to her cheeks, and he hoped that was a good sign.

He made a show of giving her his arm, and she smiled, looking at him out of the corner of her eye. It had finally happened. He was at an event with a beautiful girl, and he wasn't counting down the minutes to when it would all be over.

eg tried to tell herself that Parker holding her hand meant nothing, or that the kiss didn't simmer her insides. Meanwhile, every nerve seemed to fire from her appendage, sending tingles throughout her body. His kisses made her lips feel like she'd been eating one of those cinnamon bombs she could remember from her childhood.

But this was the gala, the biggest key to getting investors aboard with her company. As much as she wanted to stare at Parker the rest of the night, she knew she had to focus and be the CEO of Love, Austen on this of all nights.

The room was near full, and she nodded at several people as she walked over to a microphone in the corner. The dancing and desserts would be in the next room over, but she'd wanted a way to greet the guests. Tiffany gave her a nod, and she stepped up to the microphone, ready to begin.

"Welcome to our Love, Austen family. We're so excited to have you tonight. To all our guests, we hope you enjoy the food and the dancing, and that you have fun tonight. For any of the friends who're with us for the first time, please don't hesitate to ask any questions. We're here to help your dreams of love come true. It's something we're passionate about.

"You should have received your table number in our last email to you, but if you forgot it, please see my assistant, Tiffany, and she can direct you. For the newest clients, you're seated with one of your matches for dinner and then should have the other two matches on your dance card later.

"Go ahead and get comfortable. Chat with old friends and make some new ones. The food will be out shortly, and then we can dance the night away, Jane Austen style!"

The room erupted with applause, and the people moved to take their seats.

Meg and Parker sat near the back of the room, sharing a table with three married couples, one of which was Lily and Ben. The other two had been matched during Meg's second year with Love, Austen, and had both married within the last year.

As she studied them, she couldn't help a thrill run through her. This was what she needed tonight, to see that no matter what the investors decided, she was making a difference in people's lives.

"What are you thinking about?" Parker asked as they ate their main course.

She gave him a bashful smile. "Just how exciting it is to see people happy because of something I built. I didn't ever imagine we'd be at this point."

"It's definitely something you can feel good about. My job, on the other hand, not so much." She saw the vulnerability flicker again, and she moved her hand to where his rested on his leg.

With a squeeze, she leaned closer, breathing in a smell she couldn't quite place, but it tantalized her all the same. "You put a lot of work into it. And there have to be people who appreciate it. But if it's not something you want to do anymore, make a change."

He gave her an unconvinced smile, and they continued to eat, joining in the conversation of the other couples.

Lily turned to her. "You look amazing, my dear. Pink suits you a lot better than teal."

"You're a couple of weeks late with that assessment, but I think you're right." They giggled together, and it was refreshing to be surrounded by so many good people.

She snuck a glance at Parker, and her stomach did a somersault. She'd fallen fast for her fake boyfriend, and she hoped he felt the same now that her brain had finally accepted the fact.

With dinner cleared, the guests made their way into the ballroom. Two long tables were set up against one wall, boasting the pastries and cakes she'd seen in the kitchen earlier. She'd already received several comments about the food and now as she walked by several guests sampling the desserts, gratitude flowed through her once again.

"Would you care to dance, m'lady?" Parker gave her a teasing grin, and she thought she'd melt standing right in front of him.

"I should probably check—"

"Just one song. Besides, you're in the spotlight tonight. Dance the first dance."

She eyed him again before reaching out and putting her hand in his. With his hand on her upper back, guiding her toward the dance floor, an electric pulse shot out across her shoulders, and she shivered.

"Are you cold?"

She shook her head. "No, just getting out some jitters."

They moved into the center of the room, the string

quartet playing a rendition of the song on the newest *Pride &* *Prejudice* movie. Parker moved her forward, backward, and then to the side, making her feel like she was dancing on a cloud. The ballet slippers made her feel graceful and as he spun her and then dipped, she felt her heart speed up as he paused, looking in her eyes.

Before she knew it, the song ended. The applause echoed off the walls, and the musicians began the next song. Parker tightened his hold on her, and she assented to his unspoken question, until they turned, and Tiffany caught her eye. Meg didn't like the look on her assistant's normally easy demeanor.

"Tiffany needs me. Will you dance with me when I get back?" She searched those pool-blue eyes and figured she could lose a lot of sleep just staring into them.

Parker's smile made his eyes squint. "Of course. I can come with you if you need."

"I should be okay." Her gaze lingered on him for a few backward steps before she turned and hurried over to Tiffany.

"What's wrong?"

"We have an issue with a woman trying to come into the ball without an invitation. She's causing quite a scene, saying she's your mother."

Why of all nights would she decide to show up here? How did she even know about it?

Meg held up a hand. "I'll handle it." She walked in the direction of the main door, wondering what kind of scene she'd find this time. Stepping past the ushers at the door, she looked around the hallway, trying to see where the woman had gone.

"Margaret, darling. What a wonderful event. Pity I wasn't on the guest list."

Closing her eyes, Meg turned on her heel to see Virginia

Greyson, in all her glory. Her usual blond hair was dyed a strange shade of red, purple accents shining through. She was dressed as if she were going to a Hollywood award show and not for a Regency gala.

"Mom? What are you doing here?" The clipped words surprised her, but tonight wasn't the time to be dealing with her love-seeking mother.

"I heard about a great party being held here, and your company was throwing it." Meg knew the mock-innocent tone well, and she tried to think of a quick way to solve the situation without making a scene. Nothing was coming to her. She couldn't just have security haul her own mother away, although she'd like nothing more.

Meg searched around behind her mother. "Where's Gerald?"

"We weren't right for each other, dear. I'm a single lady once again, and what better place to find a new match than at my daughter's matchmaking ball?" Her eyes flicked to the room behind, fluttering her eyes a little more. Meg turned to find Parker standing like a bodyguard behind her. Virginia's seductive smile made her look more like the Cheshire Cat. "Who might this dashing young man be?"

Feeling all the exasperation of a frustrated teenager, Meg said, "This is Parker Matthews, my date."

"Aren't you delicious enough to eat? Are you from Boston?" Her mother rested one hand on his upper arm, and Meg wanted to crawl in a hole as she saw her mother's fingers squeeze. Green tinged her vision, and she had to suck in a breath. This reeked of Carl Ashbury senior year of high school when her mother had tried to date Meg's boyfriend.

"Yes, ma'am. I've lived here most of my life. It's a pleasure to meet you." Parker's voice was cordial, but Meg saw him glance at her, concern in his eyes.

Her mother let out what sounded like a cackle to Meg.

"Oh, Margaret. It seems you finally found a respectable young man who's also good looking. Too bad I didn't find him first." She bit a fingernail as she stared up at Parker once again.

"No!" The word sounded like a bark coming from Meg's mouth. A hand touched her arm, and she turned toward Parker, worry etched into his face.

"What do you need me to do?"

Meg shook her head. "Nothing. I'll take care of it. Just go tell Tiffany to make sure we're all stocked up on the desserts."

Parker nodded, giving her a sad smile before turning and walking back into the great room. Meg turned her mother around and while smiling at the other guests, tugged her along, making it down the hall before the woman put up any resistance.

"Is that any way to treat your mother? After all I've done for you, this—"

"Enough," Meg said through clenched teeth. "I've had enough of your attitude towards me, and I'm sick of your ever-changing relationship status. Parker is an amazing guy. He read *Emma* because he knew I like the characters. He's been through so much to help me pull this off, and I won't let you waltz in here and think you're the next Marilyn Monroe."

Her mother's eyebrow raised, as if bored with the conversation. "Is that all?"

"Leave now, or I'll have you escorted from the premises."

"You wouldn't." The harsh tone in her mother's voice caused Meg to pause.

Closing her eyes and counting to three, Meg said, "If you really want a guy for longer than two weeks, stop by my office on Monday."

The expression on her mother's face softened. "You mean you'll help me?"

"I haven't decided yet. But I'm hoping that by Monday, I'll have an answer for you." She lifted her chin and turned, not wanting to break down during one of the biggest nights of her life. If she could deal with her mother on Monday, that would at least get her to leave without causing a scene.

Placing a hand on her mother's shoulder, Meg nudged her toward the door.

"I'll be at your office at eight sharp Monday morning then," her mother said. There was that excitement in her face, the same expression Meg had seen for every relationship her mother had had since her father passed away.

"Okay, I'll see you then." She watched as her mom walked down the stairs, saying hello to several couples walking toward the entrance. Guilt hit Meg. The poor woman just needed to fill the void left by her husband's absence.

Adrenaline poured through Meg. She'd managed to stand up to her mother and had also seen a different side of her. Would she be able to say what she felt for the tall brown-haired man she loved?

I love him. She'd felt the words, as if they were written on a blackboard flooding her mind. The revelation echoed throughout her body, and she felt an urgency to tell him before the walls could be rebuilt around her heart.

Scanning the side, she couldn't see him. Her gaze drifted over the dance floor, searching through the couples for Parker.

Her rambling mind went into overdrive as she looked through the crowd. Couples twirled and stepped along the dance floor, and through a break in the people, she saw him in the corner, dancing with a woman in a plum-colored dress. As she turned toward Meg, the jealousy she'd felt earlier with her mother sank into her chest.

Courtney Caldwell.

She recognized the beautiful brown tresses and curvy

figure, from her research. The woman's face was like a cherry on top and if Parker were handsome enough to be a model, in Tiffany's eyes at least, this woman would be the one draped over him in the photoshoot.

Meg watched as several men gawked at Courtney, one even getting a smack on the face for it from his dancing partner.

Studying Parker's face, she recognized the mask hiding his emotions. But what was he feeling on the inside? Was it dread? Or the awakenings of a lost love? She hoped it was the former.

The music ended on a soft note, and the dancers bowed to each other. Taking one step forward, Meg froze as she watched the woman snake her arms around Parker's neck, pulling him close as she touched her lips to his.

Paralyzed with shock, she couldn't tear her eyes away, reaching up to feel her own lips as if they felt the betrayal as deeply as her broken heart did. Although she could still hear the buzz of the room, her brain told her everyone had seen the kiss and was staring at her for a reaction.

How long was he going to let her fondle his lips like that?

The next song pulled her out of her hesitation, and Parker looked up, eyes connecting with hers, a look of horror on his face.

Holding back her tears seemed like she was holding up a dam single-handed, but this was a special night for her guests, and she didn't want to ruin it. Nor did she want to see the pity in their eyes.

As she walked to the dining room, Meg saw Tiffany and said, "Take care of things for me. I need a few minutes alone." She had to choke out the last few words and hurried to a dark corner at the other end of the dining room. Without a mirror, she knew her ugly-cry face was making an appearance, and it was better to let it run its course.

This was the second time she'd cried over a woman making advances on her fake boyfriend. Ending the agreement was the only way to mend the tiny pieces left of her heart, and she would do it. After she had a good cry.

CHAPTER 32

The moment Courtney Caldwell walked up and asked him to dance, Parker felt as though hands had encircled his lungs and squeezed together as hard as possible.

It had been three years since he'd seen her, and every feeling and emotion flooded back. The elation, the excitement, and then the crushing regret and anger. If only he'd seen her lack of commitment earlier.

"I didn't expect to see you here. Are you here with anyone?" Her rich voice called up memories from years ago, but he was grateful the emotions were no longer there.

"I'm here with the owner, Meg Austen." Balling up his fists, his breath came out in bursts. He glanced at her purple dress, the cut not right for a themed party, but he couldn't expect anything less from her.

She jutted out her hip and set her hand on it. "Well, how about a dance for old times' sake?"

What could he say? He'd gone through so many emotions in the days after they'd broken up, one of them hoping she'd come back. Curiosity won over, thinking maybe he'd get more to the story of why she'd left so abruptly, and he gave a curt nod.

As he positioned his hand along her upper back, they moved to the slow rhythm of the song. He felt strange, as though the past three years hadn't happened at all. But instead of feeling love, his heart sped up as if warning him. The feel of her hand in his was so familiar, and she looked like she hadn't changed at all. And yet, everything had changed for him. "I didn't know you were back in town."

She laughed, but Parker kept his face emotionless. "I moved back a month ago. I got a job at my uncle's firm, and I've secretly been hoping I'd run into you somewhere."

Parker didn't take the bait, focusing on the steps and the rhythm of the music. He could feel her staring at him, but he avoided her gaze, looking out to the other couples on the floor.

"How are things at your father's firm? I'm so sorry to hear of his passing." He looked to her then, surprised to find a soft expression on her face.

"Thank you." He bit the words out and took a breath to calm himself. Anger coursed through him now, and all the arguments he'd concocted in his mind with her over the years seemed to fight with one another. He pushed them back. "We are doing well. I'm up for partnership."

"That's great. I knew you would be someday." She fluttered her eyelashes a few times before saying, "I'm sorry, Parker. I made a huge mistake, and I really wish I could do that day all over again."

Not trusting his eyes to look at her, he looked to the string quartet and asked, "What would you have done differently?"

Out of the corner of his eye, he could see a deep frown, a line forming in her forehead. "I would have let you propose." She paused and then said, "And I would have said yes."

Parker's eyes snapped down to hers, searching them for the punchline. When he found none, he said, his tone rough, "You're telling me this three years later?"

Parker heard the music slow down, grateful for the end of the song. He let go of Courtney, and she stepped closer, wrapping her arms around his neck and kissing him. It held no passion, and after a few seconds, he pulled back. It was nothing like kissing Meg.

Meg.

Panic buzzed through him as he searched the side of the dance floor. Every pink thing caught his attention until he saw her diagonal to them on the dance floor. Defeat caused her shoulders to round in, and her eyes narrowed, their hardened look sending daggers toward him. She turned and disappeared into the crowd.

He broke away from Courtney and tried going after her, but she was too fast. After a few minutes, he found Tiffany.

"Have you seen Meg?"

"She said she needed a few minutes alone. Is everything okay?"

Parker ran his hand through his hair and over his face. Why was this happening today?

"Tiffany, I'm sure I love her. This started out as an agreement for a fake relationship, but I feel so much more for her. I can't lose her."

Her face scrunched up, as if looking at a cute puppy. She said nothing but pointed into the dining room, where only a few lights were still lit.

"Thank you. A million times, thank you." He rushed off into the room, waiting for his eyes to adjust to the light.

"Meg. Meeeg. Please talk to me. I need to tell you something."

He called out a few more times before hearing a sniffle from a dark corner. Taking long strides, he saw her leaning against the wall next to a cart of chairs. "What are you doing here?"

She sniffled again and whispered, "Wondering why I ever agreed to be your fake girlfriend. I've been through so much when it comes to love, and I thought there was no way I could get hurt, especially from a fake relationship. We're done, Parker. Now you can get back together with that tramp and not have to feel guilty."

The coldness of his name on her lips pierced his chest. "No, please don't do this. You don't understand."

"I guess that answers my question. I just never thought I'd get it." Her frown deepened. "Please, just go."

"What question?" His words were clipped as he felt frustration surge.

"My question about if you'd ever get back together with her."

Running a hand through his hair, he held onto his neck, not sure whether to stomp away or pull her into his arms.

"I'm not getting back together with her."

Meg shook her head. "Do you think I'm an idiot? I watched her kiss you, and you didn't pull back. I can't go through this right now. I don't care if I don't get the investment. I—just go."

He opened his mouth, ready to confess everything, but the look on her face told him she wouldn't believe it, not now anyway.

"Someday, I hope you'll realize how much I… how much I care about you." He turned and walked away, almost jogging as he left the building and out into the balmy night.

He wasn't sure where to go or what to do. As he replayed the words, had he missed the signs again? Had she ever cared about him? She'd kissed him at the apartment. Her flirting and long looks in his eyes. She had to have felt something.

She'll never break down those walls. You can't get in. The thought was like a shadow over his heart. He could build some of his own. He wasn't going through the same things he had with the other women who'd abandoned him. This time, he was saying enough.

Instead of turning to get his car, he walked the six blocks to his office. The movement felt good, and it gave him time to cool down. Enough to focus on the cases Bart had given him. And he'd have to use every spare moment to do that, because he would get that partnership even without a significant other.

The signs were all there. She was one foot out. It was time to lock his heart for good.

Meg's body felt the exhaustion of the past few days, but none of it matched the pain in her chest. How could she have fallen for him? Was she turning into her mother? After all the careful planning and guarding of her heart, she should've realized he still held a torch for his ex. But that's just how her luck went.

They cleaned up after the gala until one in the morning, and she was grateful for Lily and Ben driving her home. But as the sun came up, she stayed in bed. She couldn't get out of her mind the image of that other girl kissing Parker. She was the one who got away. Meg couldn't compete with that.

His last words played on repeat in her mind. Next to the image of their kiss on the dance floor, it seemed she'd tricked herself into thinking she loved him. She'd fallen and hard. Getting out of the emotional tunnel she'd thrown herself into wouldn't be easy. But man-vegan was her new motto.

She slept fitfully Sunday night and called Tiffany the next morning, telling her to cancel her appointments. She did the same for the next two days, only texting this time.

By the time Thursday dawned, she knew she couldn't stay

in bed forever. And as wonderful as Tiffany was as an assistant, she still had college to worry about. Final exams were coming up and even though she hadn't said anything, Meg knew her stress levels were increasing daily.

After ordering a large Nutella hot chocolate at The Creperie, Meg walked into the office, giving a bleak smile in Tiffany's direction. She knew she should talk to her, but she needed a few minutes alone. Shutting the door, Meg waited for her computer to start.

There were over a thousand emails in her inbox, and she scanned the headlines for the most important ones.

Her eye caught on one from the Boston Investor's Alliance. Clicking on it, she skimmed through. Some of their members would be gone the following week, and they wanted to do a review meeting that day. Glancing at her watch, Meg saw she had four hours until the meeting.

Should I even show up?

The chances of getting any money from them now seemed bleak. She had been hiding out in the corner for so long at the gala, she wasn't sure she'd even met any of the investors.

Her eyes drifted to the picture of her and Parker next to the Bunker Hill Monument. Their cheeks were rosy, and a light sheen of sweat shone on their faces. The insane number of steps up into the tall tower, coupled with the tight quarters and humid day had taken it out of them. She slammed the picture down, so she couldn't see his smile or his eyes or anything that made her feel.

An hour later, an appointment Tiffany had set came in.

"Meg," Tiffany said at the door. "This is Courtney. She's ready to find a match." Tiffany smiled at Meg, her eyes showing concern.

Trying to fake the enthusiasm she hadn't felt in days, Meg stood. "Come in, Courtney. Please take a seat." It wasn't until the woman sat down that things clicked in place. This was Parker's Courtney. Why would she be here?

She felt a tension heighten in the room, but Meg wasn't sure if the other woman felt it too.

"Tell me about yourself, Courtney." Meg intertwined her fingers and rested them on the desk. *What is she doing here? Gloating?*

"I'm single, twenty-nine, and I'm looking for a lasting relationship." The woman smiled, and Meg grabbed a pencil from her desk, squeezing it. "I moved back from Seattle and after your gala on Saturday, I'm ready to go all in."

Meg's lungs burned, and she wondered if it was possible for steam to shoot out her ears, like she'd seen on cartoons as a kid. "What brings you to Boston? Are you from here originally?"

Courtney shook her head. "No, I grew up in D.C. but came here for law school. When graduation came around, I received an amazing offer from a firm out there. But it got old, and I came back to practice at my uncle's firm here in the city."

"Is there any other reason you came back?" Meg tucked her lips in, waiting for any mention of Parker.

"Honestly, I dated Parker during law school. Over the past few years, I've wondered what my life would've been like had we gotten married. I guess part of me came back to see if there were any sparks."

Meg lowered her gaze and leaned back in her chair. "And what did you find?"

"That he's already in love with someone else. You."

Snapping her gaze up to look at the woman, Meg narrowed her eyes, studying every bit of the expression on Courtney's face.

"Then why did he kiss you?" Standing, Meg pointed the pencil at Courtney.

Courtney's eyes flew open. "I kissed him. He didn't kiss me back."

"What?" Meg asked, slunk down in her chair, unsure how to feel now.

The woman's mouth opened, and it took a moment for words to form. "I came back and was hoping to run into him. I saw your segment on *Everything Your Heart Desires* and figured if he saw me again, he'd realize he still loved me." Courtney fiddled with the snap on her purse.

"So, you decided to crash my gala to take him from me?" Meg had never heard such a harshness in her voice, but it seemed like the acts of betrayal just kept coming, and she needed to release some of the anger.

"When we danced, he wouldn't so much as look at me. The kiss was my last effort to win him over."

Taking in another breath, she said, "I found him at his office after, surrounded by piles of paperwork. On a Saturday night. I told him how sorry I was, that I shouldn't have tried to go right back to where we left off."

Meg kept her breathing shallow, hoping to hear every single detail over her pumping heart.

"He told me he no longer had feelings for me, and that every woman he ever loved has left him." Courtney gave her a pointed look.

"That doesn't mean he loves me." Meg's voice didn't have the anger she'd hoped it would. "I was his fake girlfriend, there to help him get the partnership. It was me who misread everything."

Courtney shook her head. "No, he's trying to protect himself. Do you like him?"

Meg did a quick inward search and found her pulse spike. "I did. Now I don't know how I feel."

The two women locked eyes, and Courtney asked, "Do you love him?"

Tears erupted like a spring, cascading down Meg's cheeks. "Yes." She reached for a tissue from the box on her desk and dabbed at her eyes.

"Then tell him. Now. If you want any kind of future with him, don't wait three years and hope he still cares."

Letting out a laugh, Meg said, "Some matchmaker I am. I should be the one telling you what to do."

Leaning forward, Courtney took Meg's hand. "I wish I had someone to give me a pep talk years ago. Go talk to him. I'll set up another meeting with your assistant, and you can help me find my own knight in shining armor."

Meg could feel her heart thrum, and she looked down to see if her chest had expanded as her heart seemed to agree with Courtney. She'd already missed the time she spent with Parker. After looking at her phone every few minutes for the past few days, hoping he'd send a text or call, she felt a flicker of hope.

"I told him to go away. Why did I do that?" Meg stood, running around the desk, and gave Courtney a hug. "I love him. I've got to tell him." Running out of the office, she said to Tiffany, "Help Courtney take the test for now and schedule time tomorrow to meet again."

"Where are you going so fast?" Tiffany gave her a crazed look.

"To tell him I love him." Meg could hear the faint shriek of excitement as she ran down the street to the nearest T-stop.

She fidgeted on the train, unable to sit still. What she wouldn't give for the whole thing to turn into a bullet train, stopping right at his building.

She got off the train at Government Center, and she moved to the platform for the blue line. Looking to the board above, she saw the next train wouldn't be there for another ten minutes.

His building was near the New England Aquarium, almost diagonal to where she was now, or so her map app told her. Turning, she ran up the stairs and out into the humid April air. Smoke from a passing car caused her to cough, a wheezing sound coming from her throat. Pulling out her phone, she waited for it to recalculate and took off in the direction it told her to go.

After a block or two, she slowed from a sprint to a jog. As much as she wanted to get there in a few minutes, she didn't want to be confessing her love as sweat poured down her face and back, or so she told herself.

What will I say? Her brain couldn't hold onto a thought long enough to judge if it were good or not. How was she to apologize?

As she neared his building, she hesitated. Would he even listen to her?

She walked into the lobby and nodded to the receptionist.

"I need to see Parker Matthews. I'm his… girlfriend." The word came out choked, and she crossed her fingers the girl wouldn't notice.

"Okay, let me see if he's in." The girl picked up the phone and dialed a number. Meg leaned over the counter and pushed the button to hang up. She could feel adrenaline take over as she gave the girl a sympathetic smile.

"Yes, but I want it to just be a surprise, if that's all right." She winked at the young girl, hoping to convince her.

"Go on up. Best of luck to you."

In the elevator, she could have sworn that jumping beans had taken over her stomach. Concentrating on the airflow going into and out of her body, she watched as the numbers rose floor by floor until it reached the fifteenth. The clanging of the doors called loudly in her ears, and an older woman smiled at her from behind a desk.

"I'm looking for Parker Matthews' office."

The woman nodded. "Down this hall, third one to the left."

Meg smiled, focusing on each step forward as her mind told her to flee. She had to do this. If he didn't love her, then at least she would know. She was done playing games, and this was the best way to leap.

She pushed open the door to his office, imagining the look on his face as she stood there. It was empty.

"Are you looking for Parker?" A woman stood behind Meg, her arms full of file folders.

"I am. I need to speak with him right away if that's possible." She looked down and saw her hands twisting together. Dropping them to her sides, she pushed her chin up, trying to come off confident.

The woman frowned. "He's in a meeting in the conference room down the hall. You can wait here until he's done."

"When would that be?" Meg could feel herself losing her nerve.

"At least an hour. He's in with clients." Meg pushed past the woman, retracing her steps with more determination than she'd had in days.

"You can't go in there. It's a closed settlement." The woman's voice grew softer and softer as Meg put as much room between them as she could.

Seeing the conference room through the wall of windows, Meg held her breath and opened the door. Four sets of eyes turned to look at her, three curious, one annoyed. She turned to look at Parker and saw anger there.

"I apologize for interrupting, but I had to say this before I lost my nerve." Swallowing hard, she stared at him, his ice-blue irises sending a shockwave through her body.

"Parker, I'm so sorry. I shouldn't have pushed you away, and I should have let you speak. There are a lot of things I regret in my life but none more than pushing away the person I've come to love.

"I came here hoping what I've heard is true. Courtney came to my office." She saw a flicker of confusion before continuing, "She explained the whole thing about how she kissed you, and you didn't kiss her back. Oh, I'm rambling."

A man in a suit on the other side of the table said, "Can't this wait? We're in the middle of a long settlement, and I don't have time for this." He looked like the attorney for the husband.

Ignoring the man, Meg turned back to Parker. "I've loved every moment we've spent together. So, while this is the scariest thing I've ever done, I just wanted to say, Parker Jeffrey Matthews, I love you."

She felt her lips trembling and bit down, waiting for a response. Seconds passed, and she studied him, waiting for some signal he loved her back or that he could forgive her. The others in the room started to move as the tension grew stronger. Her heart pounded in her throat, and Parker looked back down at his notebook and didn't meet her eyes again. There was her answer.

Swallowing past the increasing lump in her throat, Meg moved back to the door and set her hand on the doorknob. "Again, I'm so sorry for interrupting your meeting." She walked out of the room and pushed the down arrow on the elevator.

Hearing the door open behind her, her heart leapt, hoping it was Parker coming to say he loved her. Disappointment rang through her as she saw File Folder Woman.

Averting her eyes, Meg wished she could snap her fingers and go back in time. But how far back would she go? To the gala? Or to Lily's wedding?

She felt the numbness breaking through her chest and down her arms.

As she made her way back to the T-station, she called Tiffany. She could hear the excitement in her assistant's voice, and it made her feel even worse.

"Please, don't ask how it went. I won't have time to come back to the office. I'm just going to the investor's meeting from here."

"But what about all the lists and statistics you figured out?"

"It doesn't matter anymore. No boyfriend, no proof I trust my system. They'll deny my application, Tiffany. We'll have to find another solution." Meg hit end before Tiffany could try to cheer her up. She just wanted to wallow.

Is this how he felt when his mother left?

Most of the seats were filled by the time she got on the train. Holding onto one of the metal bars, she stared at the stranger in her reflection.

She'd done it. She finally found someone, but her fears and insecurities made sure she botched it up so that even a declaration of love couldn't fix it. How was she going to help others find love when she hurt so much?

Setting her jaw, she decided to be completely honest with the investors and see where all the chips fell in the aftermath.

CHAPTER 34

Parker could feel the blood thundering in his ears. He focused on the tablet in front of him, knowing all the eyes in the room were staring at him.

Mrs. O'Donnell said, "Are you deaf? She just proclaimed her love to you and here you sit?"

"No, I heard her." He bit the side of his cheek, trying to decide how he felt. "I love her, but if she's just going to leave every time things get hard, I can't put myself through that."

Aaron Openheim, the attorney for Mr. O'Donnell, said, "We're here to finalize a divorce, not talk about your feelings, Parker."

Mrs. O'Donnell shushed him and turned back to Parker. "That's just love. if you don't keep working at it every day, it makes it that much easier to leave."

Silence took over the room for several moments, and Parker tried to remember where they'd left off. But all he could think about was what Meg had said. Before he could act on anything, Mrs. O'Donnell turned to her husband.

"I've done a lot of things I regret, and seeing such love from two young people, reminds me how close we used to be. I should never have said I wanted a divorce. All I really wanted was for you to see me how you used to, to want to tell me even the littlest things about your day. I didn't feel needed anymore, and that's what hurts the most."

Before the husband could respond, Parker stood.

"Can we reschedule this meeting for tomorrow? I have a girlfriend to catch." He smiled at the woman and squeezed her hand when she took it.

"Of course. Go catch her."

As he ran out to his car, he dialed her number, yelling when it went straight to voicemail.

She must be on the train. Or she turned it off.

Jumping in, he turned the key in the ignition and punched it, weaving in and out of cars as he drove to her office. Circling the block, he pounded his palm on the steering wheel. The closest spot was a block away.

With each pound of his foot on the pavement, his emotions followed the rollercoaster of positive and negative thoughts. She loved him. But was he too late? She loved him. And he'd sat there like a judge and jury, unwilling to bend.

He pushed open the door to Love, Austen, and Tiffany jumped, her eyes more white than color.

"Is she here?" Without waiting for her answer, he stormed back to Meg's office.

"No. She said she was going right to the investor's meeting."

"Text me the address." He was a step away from the door, breathing heavy as he hoped he'd be able to get to Meg before she went into the big meeting.

"Wait! Take these with you. Meg didn't have time to come back and get them." She stuffed a paper into the back of the file folder and handed it to him. Parker nodded and took off, retracing his steps back to his car.

Finding the address on the map, he saw the estimated

time of arrival was four forty-five pm. The meeting was set for four thirty. He'd have to gun it and hope no cops were around.

CHAPTER 35

eg sat on a chair in the lobby of the Boston Investor's Alliance. Numbness had gone to her brain, slowly building a wall around the feelings of her broken heart.

She wanted to escape, to get away from the city for a while. Everything reminded her of Parker, and she needed time away before she could be the matchmaker she needed to be. His silence when she'd confessed her feelings for him spoke volumes, but the pain in her chest was more intense than anything she'd ever experienced.

Getting away was the best option. She could go to New Hampshire. Aunt Bernice had told her at the wedding she was welcome anytime. Now was the time to cash that in.

"Meg Austen?" a woman asked at the door.

She stood, feeling like a robot on autopilot as she followed the woman through the door and down the hall-way. As she entered the conference room with the long table, déjà vu surged as her mind brought her back to Parker's crystal eyes, not blinking as she poured her heart out to him.

A man pulled out a chair for her just as she thought she

might fall, hitting the seat with a thud. Her hands shook, and she tucked them around her purse, squeezing it tighter, feeling the control drip through her veins.

She could do this. As a business owner, she'd have to push her feelings aside and give this one last shot. Straightening her back, she let her eyes bounce around the room.

Recognizing many from the gala, she bit her lip, willing the events from that night into the back of her mind. The man at the other end of the table caused her mouth to drop open and her heart to stop.

"Spencer Fry? You work here?"

"He's the CEO of our company, Miss Austen," the woman to his right said, giving her a scalding look. Meg clamped her mouth shut.

She remembered when he'd come in and asked about her boyfriend. When she'd worked to match him up, he'd been nothing but polite, pleased with how quickly she'd found him women to date.

One glance to his left hand showed a gold band on his third finger. He'd made her go to all that work for nothing? She'd accommodated his requests for much younger women and to look at him now, she didn't know whether to be disgusted or to laugh. After all that had happened today, a laugh could ease a few things.

Spencer wore a soft expression and said, "I do work here. Like Mark Allred said when he called you, we like to be thorough with our clients."

Meg looked down at her hands. "Well, Mr. Fry, I just wanted to say thank you so much for allowing me to apply. One of the stipulations you had for me was to back up my process with a significant other of my own.

"The day after receiving your call, I met someone as disinterested in love as I was but needed a girlfriend to receive a promotion at work. We created a fake relationship, hoping that it would fulfill your requirements." She looked up through her eyelashes, ashamed of what she might find. His expression hadn't changed.

"I had my suspicions about it, but I saw everything unfold with your date at the gala.."

A sinking feeling took hold in her middle, and she wondered how long she could tread water before she couldn't anymore. How could she have believed something as simple as a fake relationship could have turned out so badly after the fact? She was startled to hear Mr. Fry's voice once more.

"Considering your tone, I believe there's more to your story."

"What started out as a fake relationship quickly became something more real, for me anyway. But I'm sorry to say—"

The door swung open, and Meg gaped at Parker standing there, the harried secretary standing behind him.

"I'm sorry, Mr. Fry. I told him this was a closed meeting."

"I believe he's a part of this meeting, Mrs. Checketts. Thank you."

Meg hadn't looked at him for more than a few seconds before she felt the dam break, and the water flow freely.

All she could do was whisper, "What are you doing here?"

CHAPTER 36

Parker wanted to hit himself as he walked in and saw the agony on Meg's face. It tore at his heart more than at the gala, and he knew he had a long way to go to make it up to her. Everything he'd rehearsed on the way over didn't seem appropriate now.

Holding up the file folder, he slid it onto the desk in front of the man at the head of the table. "Tiffany said you forgot these."

"You went back to my office?" He saw a glimmer of hope in her eyes and if it hadn't been for the room of people, he would have run over and kissed her right there. As he took in the number of eyes directed his way, he realized he loved her even more. How brave she'd been to barge into his settlement meeting. This was terrifying!

"I, uh, went looking for you." Parker cleared his throat and walked a few steps in Meg's direction. "I'm sorry I didn't say anything when you came to my office earlier. I'm just used to women leaving when they find it convenient or when things get hard. I didn't think I would be okay if you ever left. But when you left my office today, I felt like you took a piece of me with you." His voice faltered in the middle, but he adjusted and made sure it was strong.

"While we may not have technically been matched by your system, Meg, I love you too." He paused, studying her face, hoping for signs she would forgive him. He rushed on, knowing he had to before he stopped himself. "I think I've loved you since our dinner with Bart and Cherice. Will you forgive me?"

He waited as Meg weighed her decision. When she finally nodded, standing and moving around the table. She took one step, and he bounded over to her, scooping her up in his arms, and kissing her like a man struggling to breathe underwater.

"I'm sorry to interrupt your union," Mr. Fry said. Meg and Parker broke off their kiss and turned to look at him, a blush rushing up her cheeks. "There was one part of his speech that was incorrect."

"What?" All the words he'd said jumbled in Parker's head, and he couldn't remember any specific thing.

"According to this paper, you are matched." The two of them walked around the table to look at the paper he was talking about.

Meg pointed at the top. "This is a comparison we use when we match someone. It gives all the smaller details we've discovered and how they coincide with the other person. I'm Emma, and you're Mr. Knightley, Parker." She hesitated before squaring her shoulders and looking the man in the eye. "I'm sorry to tell you, Mr. Fry, I think my assistant manipulated the answers to make it look like we were matched."

The older man smiled at them, holding up a small Post-It note. "I don't think she changed anything." He held out the note for them to look at.

Parker read aloud, "'These results are real. I didn't change anything. Tiff.' What did she mean by that?" He saw the color deepen on Meg's face.

"Remember when I asked you to take the test? I said I'd have her fix it, so we matched." She pointed to the words on the note, and a chill shot down his back.

Meg stood, looking at the man at the head of the table. "That's great for us, but I don't see that helping my case here with you, Mr. Fry."

Parker watched as a sly smile crept over the man's features.

"Normally, I don't condone lying to prove a point or receive money from my firm. But, what I think is rather fantastic, is you proved the point without meaning to."

"What do you mean, sir?" Parker put his hand on the small of Meg's back, hoping to give her support. Now wasn't the time to be catching her if she fell.

The man turned his chair toward them, and Parker heard several people around the table shift, curious as to what the man was getting at.

"When you agreed to the fake relationship, you were someone random at the time, right, Mr. Matthews?"

Parker nodded. Meg turned to look at him, her eyebrows drawn together in confusion.

"You took the test. The two of you dated, and you ended up with feelings for each other. Now you find out, after the fact, that you were a match from the start. Proof that your process works."

The room exploded with sound, the people talking animatedly around the table. After a moment, the man raised his hands, and the board members grew quiet.

"I would like to propose that this application be granted. Can I get a second?"

"I second," came a voice from the middle of the table.

"Board, a show of hands for?" Every hand raised.

He felt Meg's body shift, and he sidled up to her, throwing his arm around her shoulder. Wrapping her arms around his waist, she hugged him like she'd never let go.

The head man stood, reaching his hand out to Meg. "Congratulations, young lady. We'll send over the paperwork tomorrow. All we ask is regular communication on the progress of the app." They shook hands, and he leaned in further. "My son thanks you for his matches. My wife and I owe you more than you know."

Meg's mouth dropped open as he winked at her, and she threw her head back and laughed.

"Did I miss something?"

"Yeah, it looks as though Mr. Fry posed as his son to test our matching system." She turned back to him. "No wonder you wanted younger girls. When I saw your wedding band, I assumed you were a cheater."

The man shook his head and smiled. "Just a father trying to get his older son to grow up and find someone to start his life with."

Walking out of the room, Parker felt lighter than he'd felt in years. Just as they reached his car, Meg turned and asked, "When do you find out about the partnership?"

"I'm pulling out of the race for partnership."

Meg frowned. "Are you sure? Isn't it what you've wanted for a while?"

"Yeah, but I've made up my mind. I'm done watching people fight as they end their marriage. Mrs. O'Donnell said something after you left that hit me. All she wanted was for her husband to share his life with her, even the little things."

"So, what will you do?"

"I've always been interested in patent law. What do you say to giving me some pointers on being a self-employed business owner?"

Reaching up, she gave him a peck on the lips. "I'd love nothing better."

Her smile warmed every part of him and as he gazed at her, he couldn't believe she loved him. Wrapping his arms around her back, he picked her up, pressing his lips to hers. He pulled back and smiled. "I love you, my Emma."

"I love you, my Mr. Knightley."

EPILOGUE

Two months later

"There are so many people here. Are you sure you want to stay?" Parker was leading her in and out of blankets and chairs, people trying to save space on the long strip of land along the Charles River.

"I can't believe you're from Boston and have never enjoyed the fireworks from the Esplanade," Parker said.

"As much as I like people, I like them in much smaller doses." She giggled, and he threw her a smile, still tugging her along. "Where are we going?"

The sun had nearly set and by the looks of things, these people had been sitting out in the heat all day. She saw some of them eye her and Parker as they walked closer to the edge. Probably ready to fight if they decided to take the saved spaces.

Parker waved to someone, but she couldn't see around him, not minding since the view of his backside was still as

193

delicious as the first time he'd walked across the reception hall to his table.

She heard Lily's voice and ran to meet her friend. Ben looked like he'd been fending off people all day. His hair mussed, and his shirt wrinkled, an odd contrast to his normal neat and tidy appearance.

"It's about time you got here. I need a bathroom break." Ben stalked off in the direction Meg and Parker had just come.

"Hurry, dear, or you'll miss them!" Lily called out. Focusing on Meg, she said, "Then I'll never hear the end. What have the two of you been up to today?" She winked at Meg.

"We were looking for properties for Parker's law firm. Who knew there were so many options when it came to commercial real estate?"

Lily gave her a look. "You do. Didn't you go through all that a few months ago?"

Meg giggled. That seemed like a lifetime ago. "Well, I'll enjoy it more when I'm not the one making the final decision."

"Did you look at any houses?"

"A couple, just for fun. Why?"

"For starters, you could use a new place. Closer to the office even. At least you finally broke down and bought a car."

Meg grinned and pulled Lily in for a hug. She'd worried things would change once Lily and Ben married. And they had for all of a week. But one of the perks of having a boyfriend—a real boyfriend—wasn't feeling like the third wheel all the time, and Meg liked that fact.

The sky turned black, and people buzzed around them. Ben made it back just as the first firework shot into the sky, lighting it with a brilliant red. The Boston Pops orchestra played in the Hatch Shell stage to their right, the beats syncing with the pops of the fireworks.

Meg's eyes stayed riveted on the sky, filled with such wonder at the beauty of it all. "Why have I never seen this before? It's beautiful." She reached for Parker's hand, finding only air.

Turning, she found him down on one knee, ring box out. "I know we've only dated a few months, but I love you. 'Marry me. Marry me, my wonderful, darling friend.'" His voice cracked on the last two words, and Meg bit her lip to keep from crying.

The noise above was deafening, and she could only whisper, "Yes."

He must have read the answer on her lips because he pulled the ring from the box, a delicate gold band with intricate weaves. The diamond reflected the light from the fireworks above.

Once it was on her finger, he stood, slipping his hand behind her neck, cradling it gently. His lips caressed hers, and the energy bouncing between them felt like their own rockets.

She pulled back a moment, gazing into his blue eyes. "'Mr. Knightley, if I have not spoken, it is because I am afraid I will awaken myself from this dream.' I am the luckiest girl in Boston."

With a sly smile, he asked, "Have you been planning that?"

Touching her hand to her cheek, she felt the warmth. "Maybe a little bit. I had to be ready."

Holding onto each other, they stared up into the night sky. The scene was beautiful above, but she couldn't concentrate as she felt the rise and fall of her fiancé's—she had a fiancé! —chest on her back.

Turning, a smile quirked at the sides of his lips as she

closed in, peppering him with featherlight kisses. She could kiss him from now until they were old and grey.

As the song ended from the orchestra, Meg pressed her lips to his, never wanting to let go.

* * *

Lexi and Brennen's story continues in *Austen, Party of Two*

* * *

Thank you for reading *Love, Austen!* If you enjoyed it, I would love to see a review from you. You can also subscribe to Britney's newsletter here:
Subscribe to Britney's List
Or join her Facebook Reader Group

ALSO BY BRITNEY M. MILLS

The Love, Austen Series

Love, Austen

Austen, Party of Two

Austen Unscripted

Matched, Austen

Austen, Edited

The International Billionaire Series

The Australian Billionaire

The French Billionaire

The British Billionaire

The Vegas Billionaire

The Italian Billionaire

Rosemont High Baseball Series

The Perfect Play

The Perfect Game

The Perfect Catch

The Perfect Steal

The Perfect Hit

Christmas at Coldwater Creek Series

Love in a Blizzard

Love in the Lights

Love in a Snapshot

Love in the Details

Sage Creek Small Town Series

Loving His Flower Girl

Loving His Reporter Girl

* * *

Join Britney's newsletter

Get the latest updates on new releases and other fun tidbits!

www.ingramcontent.com/pod-product-compliance
Lightning Source LLC
Chambersburg PA
CBHW021331190726
48288CB00003B/1061